The Final Clue

By

E.M.A. Robertson

~~~

Dedication

To my children Jan, Alison and John with love…
…and to my God

The words are taken from the book of the Prophet
Isaiah Chapter 40 verse 31

'they shall mount up with wings as eagles; they shall run and not be weary'

Also Age UK whose team of IT instructors at Malvern have helped me hone my knowledge.

Copyright © E.M.A. Robertson 2022

First published in 2023 by E.M.A. Robertson

The right of E.M.A. Robertson to be identified as the author of the work has been asserted herein in accordance with the Copyright, Designs and Patents Act 1988.

All rights reserved. This book is sold subject to the condition that it shall not, by way of trade or otherwise, be lent, resold, hired or otherwise circulated without the publishers prior consent in any form of binding or cover other than that in which it is published and without a similar condition including this condition being imposed on the subsequent purchaser.

Contents

The Final Clue	1
Chapter 1: Opening scenes	1
Chapter 2: Run up to Grand Prix	7
Chapter 3: 1935 Grand Prix	11
Chapter 4: War clouds over Europe	20
Chapter 5: Hedge cutting and other duties	23
Chapter 6: Racing Gramps' Bugatti	26
Chapter 7: Visit to Vineyard	30
Chapter 8: "E" comes to England	33
Chapter 9: Village Show uproar	40
Chapter 10: Getting a driving licence	42
Chapter 11: Scrapbook	44
Chapter 12: Bugatti time trials	51
Chapter 13: Alterations on Farm	54
Chapter 14: Christmas 1937	56
Chapter 15: Revenge at the Village Show	58
Chapter 16: Tourist Trophy	62
Chapter 17: Confined to bed	65
Chapter 18: Dunlop come to the Park	68
Chapter 19: Breakdown	73
Chapter 20: New Land	78
Chapter 21: Telephone comes to the farm	83
Chapter 22: Resurrecting The Lorry	87
Chapter 23: Black Market Operations	91
Chapter 24: Dads Army	97
Chapter 25: Mr. Fix It	101
Chapter 26: Evacuees	107
Chapter 27: Rationing	111

Chapter 28: Near Miss	115
Chapter 29: Career choices	120
Chapter 30: Then it was over	125
Acknowledgements	131
Roll of Honour	132
Summary for book	134

The Final Clue

Chapter 1: Opening scenes

Kneeling down, I felt my bones creak as I pulled gently at a parcel wedged under the bed. I gave a sharp tug and the large scrapbook slid out, however the steering wheel which had also been stored there was now jammed in the corner by the leg, and I knew that my granddaughter would be coming soon to collect the items. Perhaps she would help me, pull everything out, after all it was she who wanted to commence work on my memoirs. It was then that I remembered my mother chiding me to keep it safe and not to give to just anyone as it had been such an important part of my childhood. What was this? An old blue hat and some paperwork in my mother's handwriting. I didn't remember that, so I tugged it gently out of the rim and started to read and my heart lurched as I held it in my hand.

Suddenly the years rolled back, and the seconds peeled away at the layers of time. I forgot the home with its' cluster of inmates as we jokingly called ourselves. I was a young boy again, growing up on a Leicestershire farm. A small thin figure with my socks falling down my legs and my hair always in need of brushing, so my mum said. Ken I was called, and always the apple of my mum's eye. I liked to climb the trees in the orchard or look for eggs from the hens while my elder brother Jack helped more with the farm and its chores. Best of all I remember being able to run to meet my grandfather when he roared into the farmyard in his latest motorcar.

A mechanical machine, it was a bond that held us, and I'd dash forward into the smoke screen and climbed up over the running board into the passenger seat. Barely able to see over the windscreen I gripped the seat tightly as the smell of the leather upholstery and engine oil engulfed us.

'Ready,' said Gramps as he gave me a huge grin and he would accelerate the car away to the far end of the farmyard and spin the wheel hard and fast into one of his infamous handbrake turns. Then I remembered the first time Gramps brought the red Bugatti to the farmyard - the car unused to such treatment slithered erratically on the mud baked surface. Gramps at the last moment yanked the wheel so that we only just made it through the open barn doors.

'Wow,' I said in awe, feeling a little dazed. 'How did you manage that?'

'Not on the agenda my boy,' said Gramps grinning as our eyes accustomed themselves to the gloom of the barn. 'You alright then? Come on, let's go and see your mother, and bring that package that's tucked in the back there, it's for you.'

My eyes lit up, Gramps was a wonderful present giver, he was the best, the tops this man, self-made and one of the new nouveau riche who had started a small toy business importing toys from Germany and Eastern Europe. You never knew what he come back with from his travels.

'Did you bring me back something from the toy fair Gramps, I asked? Why don't you wait and find out?'

I held it carefully and my face shone with excitement. 'We can't have this one pushed through a cowpat, can we?' Then he ruffled my hair as he ushered me into the kitchen. The farm dogs always greeted him with an air of excitement, yapping and jostling around his legs. They always got a loving pat and an affectionate pull on the ear from gramps and if he stayed long enough a good walk over the meadow to one of the rocky outcrops overlooking the valley, one of his favourite spots where he would sit and tell me about his latest sales trip and the places he'd seen. Today the farmhouse smelt of bread, there was a good yeasty smell in the air and the kettle boiled gently on the range. Then he turned to me and asked me if I would like to go and watch some real racing with him and have a day out?

'Where Gramps?' I asked.

'Well, it's over at a place called Donington Park and a friend of mine's been telling me they are having some very good motorbike and car races there now. What say we ask your mother?' I smiled; I knew I'd be on to a winner here. Mother liked motor cars as much as I did and had often driven Gramp's car before she had married my dad and come to live in this small knit farming community. It seemed that a chance encounter had brought my mother and father together when, yet another motor car driven by my mother had broken down by the farm gates as she had to wait for the cattle to cross.

Getting together they called it and although she was a few years younger than he, she had spent her early days on a farm, and it seemed they suited each other well. Once in the kitchen Gramps turned to pull out a chair and then saw my mum coming through from the back parlour.

'Hello Dad,' she said as she embraced him warmly. 'Thought it was you in that cloud of smoke in the farmyard. Sit down and have a cup of tea and tell us what you've been up to.'

'Look mum,' I broke in. 'Gramps has bought me a new toy from the toy fair in Germany. It turned out to be a super green and brown car. Gramps said it was a Rolls Royce Sedanca. It was one I didn't have and would be great to go with the others in my collection.'

'Thanks Gramps,' I said, dancing in glee bobbing up and down, and I gave him a big hug. '

'You'll spoil him, you know you're always bringing something back from your travels,' mum said. 'Just what will we end up doing with him?'

'Well,' said Gramps, 'now that you mention it, I've asked young Ken here if he'd like to come with me to the races next weekend, broaden his horizons a bit.'

'Can I go please mum?' I asked.

'Now you just wait a minute while I hear what your grandfather has in mind, and then I'll have to run it over with your father,' said mum.
'Well,' said Gramps grinning from ear to ear, as he was about to talk about one of his favourite topics, motoring. 'I've heard there's been quite a few meetings organised at the Park in Donington these days, which is being run by the Derby and District Motor Club under a chap called Fred Craner, and they are holding a Grand Prix. Just imagine it, an international motor race right on our doorstep with some of the top drivers. You can bet Howe and Shuttleworth will be entering, and I've heard Prince Bira will be coming as well.'

'Won't it be a bit like that big Shelsley Walsh meeting that you went to a couple of years ago? I've heard you talk about,' said Mum.

'No lass, Shelsley is what's termed as a hill-climb where cars compete against a timing system from the bottom of a hill. The 'Walsh" is considered to be a good course with a steep gradient and some sharp corners. In fact, it's become so popular that drivers come from all over the continent and large crowds go to watch. My friend Rupert took me as he knew some of the officials and we found an excellent viewing spot halfway up the hill, though it became quite crowded quickly. Afterwards we drove to a little old hostelry on the banks of the river Teme a few miles away, where they had an excellent fayre and large open fireplaces. We had a corking time.'

'It's a different kettle of fish to a race circuit like Donington,' he said reflectingly. 'There the cars compete against each other on a racetrack which is over two miles long and can overtake each other. Exciting stuff don't you think. I haven't been able to find out much more yet, but I think if we set off early from the farm, we could have a good look around the paddock and get to see a close up of some of the cars. Well, I know his dad will ask if you're going to take him in that death trap motor of yours? Have you had it seen to yet? Oh, look lass, I got rid of the Jowett, the brakes were a bit unreliable and bought the little Bugatti out there. It's a real corker, far more reliable and it should get us over the boundary to where the Donington Park racetrack is. I even had a garage run their eye over it, toying myself with racing it myself one day. Ho- Ho, toying with the idea,' as he laughed at his own little joke.

'Oh, please mum, please can I go?'

'Well let's go and check out this new car first and see what it's like,' said Mum as we all filed out the back door.

Gramps was in his element. 'Just look,' he said. 'A 4-speed gear box, and this will please your dad, the foot brake works on all four wheels. It's an 8-cylinder version and gets up to a top speed of just over 70 m.p.h. I got it for a snip from my London friend Giles as he wanted to see if he could get anything larger in a saloon. It was a pity as I couldn't persuade him to take on the Jowett.'

'Well, what do you think of her?' asked Gramps.

'As long as it will get you there safely. It looks an impressive little motor, and just when do I get to drive it?' Mum enquired.

Gramps grimaced slightly and then reminded us of that cup of tea.

It was a relaxed mood in the kitchen that morning, gossip ranged from Gramps recent trip to Germany and relating how good trade had been for the model cars he was importing to how a new Chancellor appointed in 1933 called Hitler was changing things. Even introduced conscription for the Rhineland earlier in the year. When he saw mum frowning slightly, he quickly reassured her that all it meant was that he was having to sign more paperwork to get the toys out of Germany.

'More officials and paperwork,' he groaned. He obviously didn't want to give more details because he quickly changed the subject back to motor racing at the park the next week.

'What I can do is to try and get a copy of the Autocar Magazine which comes out on Friday,' he said. 'I've heard they do some good reviews on the drivers and their racing, and I reckon Donington Park will be large enough to attract their attention. We might, with a bit of luck, get some good reviews about the track and how it's rated.'

He turned to me then and said 'How about it Ken? If you want to go, I'm relying on you to do all your homework, be a good boy, and I can ask your father,' and with a twinkle in his eye he looked at mum who nodded! By the way I saw him up in the top field at Long Meadow, he should be in soon.

That was the beginning of some of the greatest days out with Gramps to the Park as we came to call it and making friends with the children who lived in a house on Park Lane. Yet little did I realise at the time that this was an era that opened an association of my relationship with motor sport and would ripple through the family.

Chapter 2: Run up to Grand Prix

I must say the following week couldn't go fast enough and I tried to run as many errands as I could for mum. I hopped up and down with excitement and I dashed here and there getting in everyone's way, so I was told later. Even Dad was surprised that I managed to find as many eggs in the nests that the hens had around the farmyard, (trying to keep in his good books.) I was the envy of some of my classmates because I had told everyone about it, and of course many wanted to come with me. Mum said no! The little Bugatti was only a two-seater and there'd only be room for two people and the sandwiches for a picnic if we put them in the back. Reluctantly I had to agree with her.

Gramps came over mid-week with some information on the forthcoming race and a press item he had been given on the track from two years back. Mum and I read it through with him over the kitchen table as we tried to work out exactly where the race took place and where Gramps and I would have to go. We had been to Castle Donington the previous year where mum had brought a new wicker basket. She could not recall seeing any signs to a racetrack, and quite frankly neither did I.

'Looking at it though, the write up seems to go into great detail,' said Gramps. 'It appears to be over to the East of the village in the grounds of a large Hall owned by the Shields family. Furthermore, the article said it had started as an idea put forward by the Derby and
District Motor Club and after a few successful motorcycle meetings been converted at an enormous cost into a car track.'

'This is really quite informative,' said mum. 'Look here it says the roads have now been widened to about 20 feet and resurfaced with tarmac and is now two miles long.'

Gramps interjected again and said 'See here they have even put the gradients of the course in. After the start the cars had to go downhill and up again, and then swing into a sharp hairpin. All in all, it sounds exciting' continued Gramps. 'I wonder if they have got any banking there, because if not it could make it difficult to drive.'

'What do you mean, difficult to drive?' I asked.

'Well, if you take a corner too fast the car could fly over the side and into the ditch, so I was once told by my friend Rupert,' said Gramps.

Dad who had just come in and caught the tail end of the conversation then grumbled something about if it was dangerous was it going to be safe to go and watch? I held my breath, but Gramps hastily assured him he'd keep a strict eye on me, and we wouldn't be going to any dangerous places to watch. (We later learnt that a driver called Templer in a Frazer-Nash during practise had shot along for 20 yards with his off-side wheels a foot in the air) but I never mentioned it to Dad.

'Look at this,' said mum to change the subject. 'There's a picture of the cars trying to squeeze under a tiny bridge and then there's another of them driving through a wooded area.'

'It's no wonder they've called it coppice corner,' said Dad taking a quick look over mum's shoulder. 'I wonder if they ever knock over any pheasants?' he chuckled.

'I think it's a bit too near the farmhouses for that,' said Gramps. 'Because just around the corner they are marked here on the map, and it says strictly no passing.'

'I should think not,' said Dad. 'How would we like cars passing our farmyard? We have got enough on our hands with that new car of yours. Don't get any ideas and bring any of your racing people over here.'

'No, you won't get anyone over here practising,' said Gramps in a jocular manner. 'They might have to wait too long to get in the place, especially if you happen to be moving your cattle across the road and holding everyone up. I tell you there was old Arthurs dray and Mrs Moppets jaunty cab when I came up the road this evening. They looked none too pleased I can tell you,' said Gramps.

Dad roared with laughter. 'That will teach you to be in a hurry,' he said. 'Though why don't you get young Ken interested in a game of cricket beats me. What with Trent Bridge just down the road from us you could go and watch a first-class county game.' Then he started to reminisce 'When will we ever get another player like George Dunn I'll never know?'

Luckily Gramps changed the subject again before we heard the saga of his 1928 innings against Kent XI. It was a story we knew by heart. However, the chatter was amicable, and mum continued to pour over the article and then she spotted an enclosure at a place called Starkeys Corner.

'Do you think this could be a good spot?' she asked gramps. 'It says you can get a good view of the racing and there will be a tannoy system so you could hear the commentator at the same time.'

Gramps deliberated and then said he thought it would be a good idea to go down to the pits if possible. 'You never know who might be drawing in sometime for a change of driver' (you could do that then).

He made it sound so exciting I hopped up and down. I then asked Gramps who he thought was going to win, Earl Howe or this foreign gentleman they call Prince Bira.

'I don't know,' said Gramps cautiously, 'and where did you hear Bira from?'

'I thought you mentioned him last week but one of my school friends was telling me that there was a write up in the Motorsport magazine about him a while back.'

'Really?' said Gramps and thought for a minute. 'Well, I've seen him on the Hill at Shelsley Walsh and he was fast then, but I am given to understand that it's hard to judge performances on a hill climb against drivers having to race each other on a racetrack.' Dad interrupted us then and said he still had some work to do, so he'd leave us all to it, racing or no racing and reached for his cap.

'Okay,' said Gramps, 'but can you tell me if you've finished sorting the cattle today, and no holdups?'

'No chance, they are all milked now,' said Dad as he disappeared out of the door.

It was those milking cows that were going to cause all the trouble later on, but little did we realise it at the time.

Chapter 3: 1935 Grand Prix

Sleep didn't come easy the night before the race, and I tossed and turned for a while because I was so excited even though Mum had insisted that I had some Ovaltine, ugh! Never-the-less I was up with the crack of dawn, and I went through to see Gramps. It had been arranged that he could come over to stay overnight so that we could make an early start, with the aim being to get there with enough time to walk around the paddock and look at the cars. Taking a peek, I looked out of the window to see what the weather was like, and it appeared a bit dull and grey, but at least it wasn't raining. By the time we got downstairs Mum had already got the frying pan on. There was a lovely smell of sausage and bacon coming from the direction of the kitchen, and Dad had already gone out to see to the cattle. I ate so much that mum jokingly told me to leave some room for the picnic hamper later!

'No peeping,' she said as I was about to lift the lid, 'there's plenty of cheese and pickles and a nice slice of the cured ham so that should keep you both going for a while. Oh, and don't get in the way of any motor cars and be a good boy for your grandfather.'

'Sure thing Mum,' I said, eager to be off as quickly as possible. Gramps then eased the hamper off the kitchen table and turned as we were going out the back door and said of course he will be a good boy.

'Come on, can't hang around all day, can we,' he said as he winked at mum.

He then secured the hamper to the hack of the car, walked to the front to crank the handle and the engine burst into life. Jump in Ken he called, and then we were off. I waved goodbye to Mum as the car went down the track and we joined the lane.

'That's good,' said Grandpa as he viewed the milking shed. 'Looks like your dads moved the cows out and got them across already. No hold ups today thank goodness.'

The lane was quiet at first but when we reached the junction to the main road, we noticed a few motor bikes going by and a motor car.

'I wonder if they were going to watch the race?' I asked gramps.

'Could be,' he said, 'but we will have to join them first to find out'.

With that he accelerated the little car into the main road. Driving along we soon caught up with a line of traffic. There seemed to be a great many people on motorcycles mainly with pillion passengers who sometimes tried to jostle their way past us in their eagerness to get there and I desperately hoped that it would not take too long. I wriggled in my seat. It was becoming quite overcast and I felt a few spots of rain. Gramps frowned and looked at me, and then said he was going to take a diversion which he hoped from memory would bring us to the racetrack via the railway station and into the Park Lane entrance as it was called. He was hoping there'd be less traffic, but we were soon reduced to a crawl again. I could walk faster than this at the moment, so I tried to count the number of motor bikes there were, but I had to give up as a lot passed us by. Some children waved to us who were sitting on a low wall that fronted a red bricked Georgian house, so I waved back. I did wonder if they ever went down to the racetrack. Grandpa was absorbed in the driving as the road seemed to be getting narrower and narrower as the trees closed in on us. Finally, we stopped, and a man came to sell us a ticket for the race. Gramps paid and then asked him about the parking.

'At the moment,' he said, 'we still have a fair amount left but the further you go into the paddock the longer it will be before you get out. We are expecting quite a few people here today.' He then waved us on. Keep your eyes out for a parking space then Ken he said. My excitement was mounting and when I turned my head I saw the Hall. It was a grand house, with lawns that dropped away to the paddock and the woods, and in the chill autumn light the long-whitewashed building with its sash windows reflected the mellow rays. I soon spotted a space and in no time Gramps had parked up.

There was an air of bustle about as mechanics, drivers and racegoers all seemed to be threading their way to various parts of the grounds and the air was being disturbed at intervals by exhaust notes of ranging vibrations.
I was glad Gramps had said we could leave the picnic hamper in the car as it certainly saved us carrying it about.

'We'll go back for it at lunch time,' he spoke. 'Come on, I want to buy a programme and see who exactly is meant to be driving.' He gave whole shilling for it, but it was worth every penny of it. There were loads of details and a rundown of the course and who was driving. Glancing through the fixtures we saw that Shuttleworth was going to be racing for Alfa Romeo, and Earl Howe and a chap called Martin were driving Bugattis.

'This looks interesting,' said Gramps as I tried to peer at the programme. 'I'd like to have a good look at Howes' or Martins' car and see if there are any differences to mine.'

'Can you do that?' I asked.

'Don't see why not,' said Gramps, 'we've still got some time left before the start of race time, judging by this map the pits aren't far away.'

By the time we arrived there was a very festive air about the place, and I saw a large marquee which had a huge sign advertising teas and sandwiches, and I could almost feel hungry again. Gramps then spotted a marshal and went to see if he could glean any further information about the race. He seemed quite knowledgeable and went on to say,

'If you're planning to walk and see a bit of the course, try between Coppice Corner and Melbourne but take care if you go down to Hollywood. You can get a real close-up view of the cars as they go sweeping around the curve but then if they jockey for position to get through a gateway which leads downhill to the hairpin it's exciting stuff. It's a bit hazardous as they don't always stay on the track,' and he laughed nervously.

'I've heard it's going to be rather crowded today as the organisers have sold a lot of tickets. Make sure you keep an eye on the young lad there as some of these cars can only be yards away when they go by. Come to think of it if you can get into the Grandstand at the starting point opposite Starkeys Corner that would be a great place and safer too. You can also follow the race on the scoreboard,' and he jabbed a finger in the general direction of the track. 'Got to go now,' he said, and he hurried off.

'We've still got plenty of time yet,' said Gramps. 'So, lets' go and have a look at these cars first'.

The paddock was getting rather crowded, and we edged our way through and found the Bugatti of Martin. He was having his mechanic check the fuel in the tank. I went forward and touched the seat and smelt the leather and was transported into a world of cars. It was very much like Gramps. Then a voice interrupted my thoughts.

'And what do you know about motor cars young man?' he boomed.

Looking up, a face confronted me, slightly tanned with the wind. The man had sharp grey eyes and sandy hair which was now slightly greased with oil.

'Well, it's very much like my grandfathers,' I said.

'Is it now or is that a likely tale?' and he ruffled my hair.

Luckily Gramps was on hand to confirm my statement and in two minutes the men were engaged in easy conversation and starting to compare notes and the performance of Martins' car, and then asked him what he would have to do if he wanted to race his car. My ears pricked up; it would be exciting if Gramps wanted to race.

'Oh, it's easy enough,' said the mechanic, 'but one of the first things to learn is that they run a tight schedule here now, and if you get an entry form for a race make sure you get it back in plenty of time. There was a right furore the other Easter when the motorcycle brigade ran a meeting. Some of the top riders hadn't got their entries in on time and they had closed the register, so they weren't eligible to race. Fred Craner who runs the meeting here was adamant and said once the deadline was passed only those who had sent their entries in could race. So, watch out, that's the first lesson to learn.' And he laughed.

'If you've never raced before though, what you need is a really good mechanic. Someone who understands about engines and can keep the car in tune for you.'

'My man Jenkins seems to have some knowledge,' said Gramps, 'but if you'd like to run your eye over my car sometime it would help.'

'At the moment, I'm fully committed to working for Martin, but I could manage a few hours on my day off, but I warn you I don't come cheap.'

'Well, what's your best offer then?' said Gramps, 'and I've come to the conclusion that there is nothing very cheap about a motor car now.'

'Well, you will be buying my expertise knowledge and experience you know,' and they started to barter over the price.

Suddenly I heard the mechanic say, 'Done deal,' and they shook hands, then quickly started arranging tentative dates when the mechanic could meet Gramps and spend a few hours working on his engine. When we were about to go the mechanic suddenly called us back and said if Grandpa was that keen to race it might be best if he tried his hand at a few trials first and get the feel of the car. {To get a bit of race craft under his belt before tackling something as big as this track racing.} It would be good experience for you. Gramps paused, grinned and thanked him for his advice.

'Food for thought,' he said, and we proceeded to make our way around the pits to view the other cars. Will you really do a trial I asked? Well it's worth thinking about and would be good experience in handling the car he said, and we walked on. Nobody seemed to mind us looking at the cars and we eventually found Lord Shuttleworths' car and he allowed me to sit in his Alfa Romeo. It was a very different machine to the Bugatti we had seen and when the mechanic realised how interested Gramps was, he went on to tell us that the cylinders were of an aluminium alloy with steel liners. By being positioned in two blocks of four it allowed them to be interchangeable. The frame which seemed very light was rigid in the front but more flexible at the rear.

This man seemed to be a mine of information and went on to tell us that the tank was mounted as part of the tail with the air pressure in it being maintained by an engine driven pump. It was beginning to sound very technical for me. I wriggled in the seat and reached out for the steering wheel.

He carried on talking but noticed me grasping the steering wheel and then explained that the seat was positioned higher than normal to allow the driver a better view of the two front wheels and where he was driving. That at least I could agree with! I was just about to get out when Gramps spotted a man going by with some photographic equipment and asked him if he would mind taking a picture of me in the car, (and even the mechanic agreed).

'Just the present we could give to your mum for her birthday,' said Gramps.

So it was agreed that after Gramps had paid him, he would be able to bring it with him and leave it at the lodge gate, so Gramps could pick it up when he next came over this way.

He then explained he was a freelance camera man, and he said the motor sport pictures were good for his business as they have top drivers here today.

'I've seen some of the cars really fly off the road coming up from the Melbourne hairpin. It's a spot known as the Melbourne rise. Just be a bit careful if you go round that way though with the young lad,' he said. 'It'll be crowded today.'

We thanked him and made our way back to Gramps Bugatti for lunch and as luck would have it secured the last two grandstand tickets to see the race.

I was sitting on the edge of my seat with excitement. It was a running start in those days with the drivers having to rush out from the pits and then jump into their cars to get away. By the time the first lap was over Farina's Maserati had gained a full 80 yard lead on Sommer, while Shuttleworth in the green Alfa Romeo was 50 yards to the rear. The rest of the cars were like a string of beads, Featherstonhaugh, Howe, Martin, Bira, McClure, Rose, Dobson, Lewis then Everitt (who was doing the first drive on Revere's Maserati.) Apparently, Lewis was driving a Riley which had been made to suit Freddy Dixons measurements and the big man found it difficult to squeeze into the machine, but he seemed to be handling it quite well despite the squash! We could hear the commentary on the tannoy system quite clearly and it told us that Charlie Martin (the man we had spoken to earlier) had had an anxious moment when braking at Starkeys corner and shot off onto the grass and turned around completely but was fortunate enough to be able to get started again immediately. Bira who then had a similar experience wasn't quite so fortunate. He lost two laps trying to extricate himself from the grass at Red Gate.

Farinas average speed after 10 laps was over 64 miles per hour which was pretty quick considering the state of the roads. Gramps thought it wasn't as quick as he could have been going, and when we watched him go past the stand it seemed as if he was just rolling around the corners and wuffling away without any effort at all. It was a bit of a blow as it kept raining from time to time, only showers so I had to turn the collar of my coat up to stop the drips going down my neck. Then I saw one of the drivers come into the pits and change over to a co-driver, you could do that then.

Apparently, he had been cut in the face by a flying stone and wasn't fit enough to drive. There was blood all down his face and it was all smeared where he wiped it with his glove. He looked in a real mess, but things became really exciting as the race went on because some of the drivers were starting to really fight for their positions. The tannoy said Shuttleworth and Bira had both come roaring down to Starkeys corner and neither man was in a mind to give way. Consequently Bira stood his ground and Shuttleworth had no option but to charge straight onto the grass and slewed around just managing to pull up in time to avoid hitting the bank.

He was in a high dudgeon about it and when he registered a protest at the pits two laps later all he achieved was that he lost his third place to Charlie Martin.

'A waste of time. Forty laps at just over 65 miles an hour and no retirements,' said the announcer, but he spoke too soon. Within minutes Farina stopped at McLean's Corner with a broken half-shaft in the back axle. At the same time the Alfa Romeo of Rose came coasting into the pits and retired with engine trouble. Two cars out of the race in moments!

'Things seem to be hotting up,' I said to Gramps.

'Just watch it,' he replied. 'There will be a few more changes yet,' and how right he was. On the 59th lap Sommer came into the pits and besides refuelling changed all eight plugs which meant that Martin was now in the lead. It was touch and go between some of the drivers now. When Sommer looked like catching Martin up and was on the point of overtaking him his bonnet straps broke and he was flagged into the pits to remove them.

Would you believe it? Four laps later he got flagged in again to the pits to replace them.

Apparently, he got really annoyed and ranted to the marshals that bonnet straps were not compulsory on the continent, and he had been unnecessarily delayed. I wondered what was going to happen next!

He was so cross about it that he over-drove the car and by the 70th lap he came slowly into the pits and when they jacked the car up they announced he'd have to retire with a broken half shaft. He was so furious he kicked the tyre so savagely and left the racetrack.

'Bad sportsmanship,' Gramps said.

The race continued with Martin still in the lead with a man named Peverill in second, Shuttleworth was third and Howe fourth. I was wondering if we'd see any more changes when the tannoy burst into life again announcing 'One of the most serious accidents yet, Dobson has crashed his Maserati at the hairpin corner and has had to retire, we believe he has only sustained mild bruising and was not seriously hurt. We'll keep you informed.'

The main trouble for the cars appeared to be arising with drivers having trouble with their brakes and Everitt and Driscoll both gyrated at Starkeys as the result of the 'stoppers' doing unexpected things. There were only 10 cars left after 250miles when Martin came into the pits for a very quick refuelling. They put in 8 gallons in just over half a minute. He then rushed off but spun at Mclean's and lost his first place in the final laps but there was quite a duel in the lower order between the two Riley's of Driscoll and Dobbs.

All too soon it was over with Shuttleworth taking the flag in his Alfa Romeo with less than a minute to spare against Howe in the Bugatti and Martin in third. It was splendid and we all stood up and cheered and threw our hats in the air as they crossed the line.

It had been an awesome race, and I turned to Grandpa and asked him if we could come again. 'It's been so exciting.'

He grinned and said, 'Sure thing, as long as my schedule allows,' and he ruffled my hair. 'Come on,' he said. 'We have to get out of here you know. But first let's find Martin and congratulate him.'

I was quite weary by the time we went for home, but Gramps stayed for supper and I was able to tell mum all about it and show her the programme for the race which Gramps had given me.

Chapter 4: War clouds over Europe

For the first few weeks after the Grand Prix, I relived some of the moments for at least a hundred times. I saw the Alia Romeo cross the line first and the crowds standing up, throwing their hats and cheering. More than anything I knew that I wanted to get involved with motor cars, but I had little contact with any machinery. Even Gramps had to go on another of his buying trips to Europe.

He was in close contact with the manufacturers of the small toys and cars that he shipped back to England and could often be away for weeks. But it was disconcerting news that he brought back with him when he did arrive. Though I didn't take much notice of it at the time.

We had all finished the evening meal and were sitting in the snug which was a small parlour off the main kitchen when he mentioned the Germans again. One of the firms he was dealing with was Jewish and they were concerned about the big changes that Hitler was making.

'Darn paperwork,' he said, 'I just didn't know where this is going to lead. We don't want another war in Europe.'

'Surely not,' said mum, 'surely not.'

Dad then expressed the opinion that he thought there was always a need for strong leadership, and didn't Gramps think he might be being hasty. 'After all we've only just really settled since the last war.'

'Well, I hope you are right,' said Gramps. 'But I am going to keep my options open. With the economy as it is I am going to diversify a little and I'm looking into the burgeoning market for wines. I've been reliably informed that a lot of the young officers are now drinking wines and that there are some restaurants in London who will pay high prices for a good Framboise. It's a rare liquor from the Alsace region. I'm planning a little trip to go down through France. Next time I go over to the continent I can bring a bottle back with me if you'd like a sample?'

'You just bring yourself back safe and sound,' said mum, 'that's all we need.'

Just then the fire crackled, and a log rolled in the basket. So Dad turned to put another one on, and the flames licked greedily around the dry bark and danced up the chimney.

'Good logs these,' said Dad. 'They burn well and have a good aroma. It's the applewood, if I'm not mistaken pruned by old Burt in the orchard last year. He's got a good eye for cutting. Come to think of it, you can give him a hand soon ken and help him get some more kindling wood in. You might even learn a thing or two. I've asked him to trim the top coppice at Tiddocks spring. One of the best woodsmen I've come across and knows how to trim the hazel stumps so that the stooks send up good strong shoots that really make a good fence. It'll certainly keep the cattle in.'

'My advice is to keep a few things in,' said Gramps, 'just in case.'

'Seriously,' said Dad, 'as bad as that?'

'Well we'll see how it goes, but I'm keeping my options open,' said Gramps. I wriggled in my seat, the last thing I wanted to do was help old Burt trim the coppice, it sounded quite boring, and I wondered if I could make plans to worm my way out of it, when I heard Dad saying to Gramps that he was thinking of investing in a tractor for the farm. Perhaps not this year, but in a year or two. My ears pricked up, as he went on to say that the shires were getting on in years and although a good working team Mr Penny over at Primrose End Farm was always talking about his new tractor.

'He doesn't seem to be able to stop bragging about it on market day, but I've yet to see it in action. Why don't you arrange with him sometime next year then to go and see it in action?' asked Gramps, 'it could be worthwhile.'

'Let me know when you are going, because if I'm around, I'd like to see it myself.'

'Can I come too Dad?' I piped in.

'We'll see,' he said, 'and only when you have helped old Burt.'

'Do I really have to Dad?'

'Yes,' he said, 'it's about time you did a bit more on the farm. What with your grandfather taking you off to the races, you'll be asking to drive a motor car next and they all laughed. I was miffed!

'What will happen to the 'Shires' then Dad? They have won best in show for the past two years. They're proud and handsome, the 'Best matching pair as I've seen for a long time',' as I mimicked the judge, and they laughed again. This time with me.

'Don't you worry m'lad,' he said. 'There's plenty for them to do for a long time yet, and I'll not see them go. They have served this farm well, and I'll not deprive you of helping to clean their brasses and harness,' and he chortled, as I groaned.

'That takes ages I,' said. But I was secretly relieved they weren't going. They were special with their shaggy manes and snuffly whiskery noses that twitched when I went to give them a carrot.

Chapter 5: Hedge cutting and other duties

Time seemed to pass by quickly and I had hoped Dad would have forgotten about the idea of my helping Old Burt with the hedging. There wasn't even a chance, once Dad made up his mind about something that was it. I can even hear him now, 'It'll do you good to be helping more on the farm my lad and pull your weight a bit. What I want you to do is to give him a hand to pick up the bits of kindling wood and it will make things a lot easier for him. Just you be thankful I'm not asking you to make bricks from cow-dung and straw. It's a practise I've not seen for a long while now,' he chuckled.

I wasn't consoled one bit, and thought it was going to be quite boring and hard work. Fortunately, mum supplied me with a thick pair of old leather gloves that would keep the thorns out and I trudged reluctantly with Burt to the field. It was one of those crisp days. With a slight keenness to the air, but as we had had no heavy frosts yet the land lay firm under our footsteps. So far, the late fall had been dry and the dead leaves underfoot still crackled as we made our way down the footpath to the outlying hedges. I tried to talk to Burt about the motor racing at Donington Park and how exciting it was, but he looked at me long and hard.

'There's nothing much that a good pair of shires couldn't do on a farm, and did I realise how lucky we were to have such two strong and reliable animals? They won't break down you know. I reckon this motor racing malarky is for the young. Just you count your blessings my lad,' he said.

I glanced away and wearily thought I was in for a long morning. However once he got going, he stripped a lot of the dead wood out fairly quickly and drove stakes into the ground. Then he hacked down some of the major branches of the hawthorn. I thought he almost cut them off, but once he laid them on their sides and interwoven them he said,

'A lot of new shoots will soon sprout up and help make a good strong fence.'

It was as he was working away that he found the nest carefully hidden in a dense thicket of the old branches we were rooting out.

'Have a look at this my lad,' he said.

It was an old nest and he gently eased away the branches from it. Inside were two eggs which were speckled and still intact.

'Will they hatch?' I asked.

'No not now,' said Burt. 'The eggs are cold, and something must have frightened the parents off, or perhaps they were killed at some stage. It takes a lot to get them to leave a nest.'

'What shall we do with them?' I asked.

'Well, I can teach you how to blow them if you're interested?' said Burt, and I nodded in silent assent and was curious about what he would say.

'I've got quite at collection at home from when I was a young lad. But the first thing you should know is that you should only take one egg from a nest at a time. We're all right with these as it's an old nest, so it took me a long time to reach fifty,' he said thoughtfully.

'Could I see them sometime then?'

'If your dad says you can, you could come round after I've finished work for the day. You'll have to be very careful, the eggs are ever so fragile and could break easily.'

'How do you keep them then?' I asked.

'I've made special boxes for then and labelled them up,' he replied. 'Started when I was nought but a young lad your age. Though it's rare now to find an egg I haven't got.'

Time went by more quickly once old Burt got talking. He was a Scots man who had come south after his wife died and now lived with his sister. He said he had worked for a Laird on a large estate and had been one of his gamekeepers. His egg collection was partly from Lock Husky where the Greylag and the Pink Footed Geese came in with the Whooper swans and the Great Grey Strike for their winter moorings. In the summer he said it all changed. and they all flew away. Then he'd find the gulls eggs, the curlew, the Goose gander and the red and black grouse. Many of these birds I had never heard of, but he seemed to be able to name all the species of the hedgerow we were working on, as well. Maybe there was more to Burt than met the eye.

'Where do I start?' I asked, curious now.

'With these two. We can take them if your careful,' and he laid them gently in his flat cap and put them down on the track by the hedge.

Over the years I did start a collection of sorts, but nothing to equal old Burt's. I was too keen to be off to the Park to watch the motor racing. Besides I was looking forward to Gramps coming over as he said on his next visit he wanted to arrange for the mechanic of Martins to come over to give him a few pointers about the Bugatti some time. That would be just too exciting to miss.

Chapter 6: Racing Gramps' Bugatti

It seemed I was destined to wait quite a while before I saw Gramps again because he had been away on another of his business trips to Europe. He had even sent me a postcard from Paris in early April, saying he hoped to see us all again in June.

June! that seemed ages away, but it would be great to see him again and I wondered if he'd bring anything back with him. My model Rolls Royce Sedanca was the pride of my collection, but it would be great to have another model to swell the numbers. Then I remembered he had told mum that he was more interested in exploring and building up a wine trade than just sticking to cars and toys. Surely if everyone liked the cars as much as I did, I didn't see why he should be bothering with all this wine business. He had also told mum that he wasn't going to put all his eggs in one basket with the unrest in Europe at the moment. Anyway, Europe seemed such a long way away, and surely it wouldn't affect us.

How wrong I was. When he did come back it was only very briefly to arrange a time with Dad so that he could set up a meeting with his man Jenkins and the mechanic of Martin's to go over the Bugatti together. It had been agreed for the following weekend. Oh boy! I could hardly wait. Dad even cleared a large space in the barn in case it rained, so we wouldn't be caught out in the wet. This was just as well because we did get a downpour later.

It was an interesting morning as I got to watch the men at work on Gramps machine and John the mechanic of Martins was really worth his salt as Gramps put it. He saw my interest as I tried to peer at things and asked me if I liked cars. Oh yes I grinned and from then on pointed out all the relevant engine parts for me and he soon established that the Bugatti, a type 30 had a crankshaft that had a speed of approximately 3800 r.p.m's, could produce a top speed of 75 miles an hour and was in very good condition. He congratulated Gramps on such a fine model, and although it possibly wasn't the best type of model for a top motor racing event, would certainly put in a useful time at trials if Gramps still wanted to have a go.

'I could put you in touch with some friends of mine, if you'd like who organise a few events at the Midlands Automobile Club?' said the mechanic.

'That's a splendid idea,' said Gramps. 'But before I do that let me ask you just how good the brakes are going to be? The whole car seems to be a lot better than the Jowlett I had. The brakes on that were just so unreliable.'

'Well with this car there's no need to worry about it. These brakes operate on all four wheels as you know. But it is activated by a cable compensated by a chain running round two sprockets on the actuating gear with the lever being connected to the rear shoes by an additional cable. It makes it all very precise as you can see here,' and we all peered into the depths of the machine to try and get a better look.

John then went on to say that with such a good streamlined body on the machine it cuts the air resistance and makes it easier to drive. This seemed quite technical to me, and I asked John if it was really important what the car looked like. So he then explained then that Seagraves car that broke the world record in 1927 had put a lot of importance on this because the shape helped it to sit on the road so that no air could get underneath and cause it to become airborne and flip over. Wow, this man seemed a mine of information and then I spotted Jack my big brother coming over to the barn to see how we were all doing.

Trust him to come nosing around now, but by this time we had checked all the oil levels and there was nothing much for him to see as John and Jenkins were putting away all the tools. He just managed to join us for a mug of tea and a wedge of mum's apple cake that always went down a treat. You could feel the scrunchy bits of apple and the rest just melted in your mouth. There wasn't enough for seconds, which was a pity as I could always eat lots of mums' apple cake if I could get hold of it and so could my brother.

John offered to give Jenkins a lift back to town on his motor bike and Gramps waved them off, wryly remarking that he hoped he wasn't going to lose his man to some racing car outfit.

I caught his hand then and we returned to the kitchen to talk to mum. It was a lot cosier in there now that there was a new range with a bigger back boiler in it so that we draw more hot water off, but I just liked to be near it. Then Gramps said he had a surprise for us, and I was eager to know what it was. It turned out that he had been to see the camera man Klemantaski on his way back from France and had picked up the photograph of me sitting in the Alfa Romeo racing car. We all peered round it to have a look. It was an excellent shot with whole car captured against the backdrop of Donington Hall. Mum was so thrilled, and she gave Gramps such a big hug, he jokingly said she would break his ribs if she wasn't careful. Then she thanked him and went through to the snug and put the picture on the mantelpiece.

'Where everyone can see it now,' she said proudly.

'It's an early birthday present,' Gramps said.

I could tell that dad who had now joined us was equally impressed after he'd been in to see it as he came back with a huge smile on his face.

'He's spoiling you all you know, what will he do next?'

'Well how about this?' said Gramps as he rose to the occasion. 'Why not celebrate a little early and let me produce a bottle of wine for supper tonight? That's if I'm invited?' he said. He looked at mum and asked her if she thought it possible to squeeze another one around the table. Mum just laughed.

'And I can produce a bottle of wine for a treat, its in the car. It'll have to be a good bottle though to beat Vera Roses Elder Flower champagne,' said Dad. 'It's been the toasting cup for many a year around here. There's a few that would like to get their hands on her recipe I can tell you.'

'Are you sure there's going to be a market for these wines you're planning to bring back?' enquired Dad. 'And I'm sure I've asked this before, but you seem to have done so well with the toys up till now.'

'Believe you me,' said Gramps. 'There's a few new venues and markets opening for wines these days especially in the motor racing circles. Did you know there's a group in London who are called the Bentley boys because they have taken to racing the Bentley Racing cars with great success on some of the European tracks these last few years? They formed something called the British Racing Drivers Club, I think it was 1928. They drive hard and fast and when they win a race like to party. Met one of them in London just before I came back up.'

'Well, you're the businessman,' said Dad. 'Next thing is you'll be buying a house in London.'

I chipped in then. 'Can I join the club Dad, this Racing Drivers Club?'

'Hang on son I think you'll have to learn to drive first,' and he laughed good naturedly. I was disappointed and tried to hide it, so I turned to Gramps and I thanked him for his postcard from Paris.

'Was it a big place Gramps?'

'Oh yes,' he said 'and it's one of the reasons why I've been away for such a long time. After Paris I drove down to a chateau at St. Tierre…'

Chapter 7: Visit to Vineyard

He continued to talk about his travels as if he had been on a great adventure. It was a long drive, but I was introduced to the owners by a friend of mine in London. The chateau belongs to a relative of his, a Monsieur Pientot who is looking to expand his business. He said he had been entertained in style by their son Jacques, who could apparently speak quite good English.

He had been taken shooting and riding in the grounds of the estate, (not that he was keen he said) but the chateau itself was beautifully spacious with views over the surrounding valley which was south facing and cultivated with vines that had made the chateau famous throughout France. From the front portico of chateau there was a wide flat stoned terrace with shallows steps which lead to a domino pattern of lily ponds.

He turned to mum then and said, 'I wish you could have been there to see it. As a water feature it really was outstanding, but what Jacques admired most was my little red Bugatti. He wanted to know all about it and what engine size it was, as he was a very keen driver himself. We then ended up racing it against his family car with a run around the estate and then really putting the cars through their paces down a long straight on the perimeter. It was quite exciting as I got the 'Bugatti up to its maximum speed.' Gramps continued, 'Firstly I was in the lead and then Jacques crept up on me and pipped me at the post.'

'Oh, I wish I could have been there to see it Gramps,' I said. He then went on in full flow to say that he was initially disappointed he had not won but it would have been a bad show to have taken the honours and beaten his host! It had made them both so dusty that they went for a quick dip in the swimming pool. It had been a bit nippy for Gramps' liking. After they made their way back to the house where Jacques showed him around the huge rooms which housed a library and a billiard table.

Of course, then the family wanted to hear all about his house in England and plied him with questions about it. Fortunately, Jacques was a good translator for his parents which led Gramps to remark on it, and Jacques then explained that he had spent some time in England with his cousin Montague.

'A spiffing good chap,' he said, 'and always partial to our cognac and wines. Loves a good drink when he's over here.' Then he suggested that when they had finished their meal, he could show him around the distillery. Grandpa had then said he would be delighted, and they walked around the side of the courtyard to the back.

Apparently, Jacques had chatted to Gramps and explained that the winery had been started as a small venture by his great grandfather mainly for house wines and village consumption. Then this had proven so popular that it had blossomed into a very thriving enterprise by the 1900's.

So much so that they had to extend the courtyard and some of the outbuildings to hold the large vats for the cognac and the liquors which had proven so popular. Jacques had then led Gramps through some huge oak doors and Gramps said it took him a few seconds for his eyes to become accustomed to the gloom after the brightness of the outside. From where he stood, he could there were rows of wooden vats which were stored from floor to ceiling. Jacques proudly told Gramps that some had been laid down for well over twenty years. Jacques then continued to say that they now had a very big operation, and the popularity was such now that they wanted to export more to England, and my contacts. Gramps for a while seemed to have been mesmerised in this other world but he then turned to mum and said,

'I couldn't tell them all my contacts. Enough to convince them though that there are new markets opening in London and the Southeast. I am going to be pretty busy for the next few months I expect, so you won't see me around for a while.'

I felt a deep hole of sadness and saw that mum looked glum.
'Cheer up,' said Gramps jovially. 'I'll be back before you know it, and I can't afford to miss any racing at the Park if I can squeeze it into my schedule.'

I was glad he said that, it was generally a surprise his visits. He'd always tell us tales of where he had been and the presents he somehow managed to bring back with him. His deep rumbly laughter which seemed to fill the house at some little joke or other. Life wouldn't be the same without him around. It was as if he caught some of my thoughts, for he looked at me and said he'd devised a project for me while he was away, I looked up and wondered what Gramps had in mind.

Gramps then went on to ask if I could keep him updated with what went on at Donington and produced a scrap book, and went on to ask if I could put in some of the press cuttings we collected from the race last year.

'And I believe you got one or two autographs from some of the drivers. What do you say, are you up to it, our Ken?' I felt a lump in my throat then.

'It was the bestest idea ever,' I said and even Mum agreed to help.

Shortly after Gramps left, I started on the first pages of the Scrapbook. Even Dad joined in and contributed by saying he could get me the Motorsport magazine regularly for me when he collected Mum's Woman's Weekly from the local stores. It turned out to be a great magazine and occasionally featured some of the racing drivers of the day. So, I gathered all the scraps and every item of reference and mum helped me stick them in the book, Stars of the book were Earl Howe, and Prince Bira because I had managed to get their autographs while Gramps when I had been at the racetrack.

Chapter 8: "E" comes to England

Gramps came to see us in the summer, and I had hoped that he would stay and we could go to see some more racing together. Sadly, it wasn't to be. Gramps then told mum that he was really busy expanding and exploring new markets. Of course, we were all please for him, {though I did wonder if there was anyone locally who could take me}. As it happened, I heard that Alex's elder brother Tom went on his motorbike to the events and wondered if he would take me. I would try and ask him next time he was around.

Back in the snug later I heard Gramps asking my parents if he could bring an Italian boy back with him and let him stay overnight at the farm. Dad was curious as he wanted to know what had prompted this strange request? And furthermore, did he really know what he was getting himself involved in, and was concerned at the thought of a child being involved? Gramps then informed us all that it was all very legitimate, and the boy would have the relevant papers from the foreign office in Berlin.

'The foreign office,' said Dad, 'what's this got to do with them?'

'It's a requirement now for people wanting to leave Germany,' Gramps then went on to say,

'The boy is Jewish, and he has been visiting his Grandparents in Berlin, and things aren't looking too good for these people now. This Chancellor, the Germans have now, Hitler, I think I've mentioned him before is getting his nose into everything and there's a lot of unrest and hatred being brewed up against these people. Once the Grandparents knew I came back to England they asked me.'

'Asked you what?' said Dad interrupting him abruptly.

'To take the lad back with me in the car to stay with his great aunts who happen to live in this area.'

'It's hard to believe that things are really as bad as that' said mum, 'and I'm worried you might put yourself in jeopardy.'

Gramps seemed to pause then said, 'It's as I've said lass, and I've also heard that there are many more people of Jewish ancestry who are applying to leave the country. He's just one of many Jews and I have been assured that his paperwork will be in order and signed out by the foreign office in Berlin.'

Dad deliberated then and asked, 'When are you likely to bring this boy here, and what did you say his name was?'

Gramps then said, 'The boy is called Etezeeo or Inzio? Look I really can't pronounce his name properly, so I've been advised to call him 'E' for short.' {Unfortunately, it was a nickname that stuck with him as I later got to know him quite well} 'Well, I'm hoping to bring him back next trip with your permission of course?'

'You just get yourself back safely Pops,' said Mum.

'Don't worry lass, I'll have it all sorted out properly and be checking the paperwork myself, for you.'

Dad then began to be more interested and consented on the condition that he was kept informed on what was going on. As he wanted to protect the good name and reputation of the family standing within the community.

Then he looked at me quite sternly and told me that what went on at the farm was strictly family business and I was not to talk about it at school or elsewhere, and did I understand. I nodded hastily; I certainly didn't want to get into Dad's bad books and shuddered.

'Yes, Dad I do understand,' and I hoped it would be enough to satisfy him.

'Okay then Ken, Okay,' said Dad.

I don't believe anyone one in the family or Gramps himself realised the extent to which the family would become involved in this operation.

Once the word got around the Jewish community, we had quite a few children staying for short periods at the house waiting for relatives to pick them up, and on one occasion had twins who went everywhere together! Gramps got himself a much larger saloon so he could carry more passengers and stored the Bugatti in the barn which mum drove occasionally. 'Taking it out for a spin,' she called it.

On one of his visits Gramps did ask Dad how the shires were getting on as he hadn't seen them for some time. Then Dad told him that he had moved them and assured him that Old Burt was keeping a good eye on them. His first job in the morning was to take down a bale of hay to the beck by the long meadow. There was an old barn cut into the overhang of a big cave for their winter shelter.

It wasn't us who ran into trouble, it was Gramps. On one of his trips back to the farm a very small girl had been pushed into the car just as he was drawing off from his pickup point and having checked all the visa's assumed, she was with the girl sitting by the door. Luckily, he was able to get over the border as some of the guards at the crossing knew and recognised his car and only checked some of the visa's. He had brought her back to the farm without realising this and he now hoped they could trace her relatives. None of the other children knew who she was.

Dad was a bit annoyed with Gramps at this but eventually agreed that she could stay, muttering that we had enough to do without taking someone in without papers. It could leave him in a tight spot with the authorities if they knew, and he told Gramps in no uncertain terms that he would like him to get it sorted as soon as he could.

Gramps reassured him he would try his best. She was such a small girl, but she soon melted our hearts and behaved very well. At first, she tagged along with Millie and tried to help and went everywhere with her, but one day she spotted Old Burt at the back door and ran over to him to hold his hand. He then asked Mum if he could take her down with him to feed the shires. At first Mum looked dubious, but he said they were such gentle giants, and perhaps they could take a couple of extra carrots with them. Mum relented then and that became something of a morning ritual for her, and somewhere someone called her Rebekah which was soon shortened to Becky {I think it was one of the Jewish children who came to the farm}.

Gramps stayed for supper one night and mum produced one of her apple pies with lashings of custard for dessert, but the best surprise of all was that Gramps had bought mum a wireless set. I was intrigued as I had never seen one before. It was like a large box with knobs and dials on it. Gramps then tried to tune it in as he put it, and he eventually found the British Broadcasting Corporation in London and then said we would be able to get the world news before it was printed in the newspapers.

Dad commented, 'When are we going to get the time to listen to it?

Once the word got around the village that we had a wireless set, some of his friends just popped in to see it and hear it working. I remember Alex was so overawed by it he would not believe me at first and wanted to open the back of it. He could be such a silly boy.

Sometimes mum allowed me to give the market a miss as Alex's older brother Tom had a motor bike. As they lived in the village, I had badgered him until he said I could go with him to watch the motor racing at the park, on the condition that I paid for it myself. This proved hard at first because I always wanted to eat my egg money by buying sweets. After a couple of visits though I made some friends with the children who lived in a large Victorian house in Park Lane. I was grumbling one day and said I'd only just enough money to come today, and I thought they were terribly lucky because they always seemed to be hanging about the place. They just laughed and look at each other and said shall we tell him?

'Tell me what?' I said.

They seemed to nod in agreement and then said, 'It's about the gap tickets.'

'Gap tickets, what are gap tickets, and how can they be any different from the normal ones? I've never heard of them.'

They looked conspiringly, Robert, Malcolm and Margaret, 'Okay then, look silly, you don't pay at all, just follow us,' and they had shown me then how they managed to do it. They had taken me back through the woods while the racing was on to a point where an old chain bridge crossed the road beneath us. Then followed a line to the footpath we were on.

'Wow, that's great,' I said. 'But are you sure it is safe, and I won't have to pay?'

'Well, it's what most of the locals around here use, and nobody is here to stop you, and once you're in, you're in. But we don't normally tell anyone as we don't want to get into trouble. Promise you will keep it a secret?'

I deferred for a moment. 'Promise,' they insisted.

'Well, it could be a bit tricky as I come to the races with my cousin on his motor bike, so it would be better if I let him in on it.'

'If you must then, but no one else,' they said.

I was curious by now and asked them, 'How come you know about it and found out you could get in this way?'

'There is not a back lane or track that we don't know of for miles around,' said Robert rather smugly. 'In the holidays we go fishing by the river at the Priest House just down from here, and there's a point where a lady will row you across to the other side. It was Margaret's friend Betsy who just happened to mention one day that some of the drivers who stay with them at the Priest House while the racing is on, sometimes walk across that way as a short cut if they've left their car in the pits. Try not to bump into any of them on your way across though,' and he laughed. After that it was much easier for Tom and me. He was not too keen at first and he made me swear not to tell my mum and Dad as he said he'd get a real tongue lashing off my old man as he put it, about leading me into bad ways.

'So, you'd. better keep your mouth shut and buttoned,' I nodded in agreement and hoped desperately that Gramps would be around for the next Grand Prix. There was another one due in October and it would be such a special day to run over to the Park in Gramp's car and let him pay! It turned out we didn't use the gap tickets for long as Tom was always asking questions and talking with the organisers of the course. He became so friendly with them that they asked him if he would like to help out at some of the events. He got provided with a proper badge and tickets for the day and as a result, I tagged along too!

Everyone thought that I was part of the set up and I was often asked to help by carrying messages from one part of the park to another, so I knew the place like the back of my hand. The Marshalls got so used to seeing me that they even referred to me as the lad.

'Ask the 'lad',' they'd say, 'if anyone wanted an errand run?' Oh boy I felt chuffed. Of course Tom had snapped at the opportunity about being a marshall but asked me to play down the events a bit as he knew his mum and dad were not keen on the idea as they thought it could be dangerous. I agreed with him as I certainly didn't want Dad getting any ideas about it being dangerous and stop me going so little was said about it at home. However, Mum became curious because I was taking home all sorts of things, old tickets, programmes and even old programmes of some of the events the drivers had been to previously. She wanted to know how I had come by them, especially the autographs. I told her then about my being called the lad as I always turned up with Tom who helped at all the events now.

Then I went on to say sometimes I would be asked to take a message from the telephone booths to the drivers and it was then I would try to get their autographs. My stack of memorabilia was mounting up. Luckily, Mum was rather lenient in that respect, and she always liked motor cars, so all she said was I should always be careful, though I guess you know your way around the place by now. I grinned from ear to ear and told her it was such a corking place to be and, 'The racing mum, you should see it, it's so exciting.' She then told me that she hoped I would develop some other interests other than the farm as my elder brother Jack would inherit it, and I'd have to make my own way in life.

'It will be tough for you Ken but if you carry on the way you are going by developing some of your bartering skills by selling some of the market produce you could be as successful as your grand-father,' and she ruffled my hair. As an afterthought she said, 'and the best mechanic in these parts.'

Chapter 9: Village Show uproar

One of the little jobs mum had lined up for me to do that year on the farm had been to help give her a hand with the vegetable patch as she wanted to give Sam Johnson a run for his money and take the local cup for the best exhibition of carrots. There had been stiff competition between the two of them for several years and the rivalry was intense. Mum grumbled that he was so well in with the committee that he seemed to think it was his right to win. She even enlisted Dad's help to find the right seeds. There were shorthorns which she had used for early sowing. The taste was said to be excellent and she also tried some called the Long Surrey which she knew would grow fairly big but had long straight roots which were said to have a good colour. She had spent hours thinning the carrots but still wanted me to put some in drills of 6 inches apart. It was like a battle plan, and everything had to be kept regularly watered.

Come the day of the show Dad hitched up the pony and trap for a good early start and Mum had washed and tied the carrots with straw and they were ready for entry. We got there in good time but as with the way of most things, nothing went to plan. The exhibits were put on display in the big marquee which had been erected in the shade of a big oak tree and then most people had gone outside to watch the children's races.

We had gone out early as I'd entered in the egg and spoon race, and mum had supplied the eggs which had been hard boiled the night before. She said raw ones would be too messy!

I was neck and neck with Rosie Bates and I thought I was going to beat her but at the last moment she lunged across and dipped low at the line.

'Pipped at the post,' they said.

I was second and Joshua Daniels came third. After that mum said she would like to view some of the stalls around the field an mum said we should make our way back for the judging and see how things were going in the big marque.

'It's my best year ever,' she said.

Well, talk about pride coming before a fall. When we got back there was a big hullabaloo on, one of the prize exhibits in the show had escaped. It was the pet rabbit of young Cyril Bakers. Although he always said he had secured it safely in his hutch it had got out and eaten some or the exhibits, including mum's prize carrots, while everyone was out watching the games.

Mum was in high dudgeon about it and went to see the remains. The organisers commented that they must have been good carrots for the rabbit to have eaten so many, but Mum was not consoled and wanted to go home to get some more carrots, but there just wasn't time. The organisers said they would declare the contest for the carrots null and void which they thought would be fair, but mum always suspected foul play. The rumours were rife for a week, and it was even suggested that Sam Johnson had bought a new rabbit for Cyril Baker. Mum was not happy going home that night and seemed to bristle for days afterwards so nobody dared mention Cyril Baker or carrots which co-incidentally never appeared on the dinner plate until sometime later.

It wasn't until a month later that Gramps came on one of his visits that the subject was even raised again. Of course, he tried to look terribly serious and concerned but he saw the funny side of things and had grave difficulty from keeping his mouth from twitching as mum told him about that "dam rabbit" of Cyril Bakers.

'It's a great shame, and I'm sure you would have won,' he said consolingly as he spluttered with a "tickle in his throat". 'But I've an idea, I'll try and make up for it.'

Mum looked at him suspiciously and rather curiously as she liked his presents as much as I did, and trying to look mollified asked 'How?'

Chapter 10: Getting a driving licence

'I've read an article in the newspaper,' said Gramps cryptically.

'It's in the car,' and he rushed out the door on the pretext of getting it. He was trying to hide his laughter.

Of course, when he came back with the news cutting he was in control, and pointed to the piece in the paper.

'Yes, here it is. A write up by the Government who are going to introduce driving tests, and licenses. It says here that if you've already driven a motor car on a regular basis or own one you can apply for a license without taking a test. I'm going down to the council offices to try and find out a little more about it next week, so shall I pick up a form for you? You can always say you've driven the family car on a regular basis.'

'Do you think I need to?' said mum, 'As we use the pony and trap on a regular basis and I'm not sure if Michael (my dad) wants to get a car just yet?'

Gramps then pointed out that he thought it would be good to get one now even if she did not use it for a while, as the test could be quite difficult and then there might be all the palaver of organising it. I had been listening quite intently.

'Can I get one as well?' I asked. 'I'd love to be able to drive a motor car.'

'Woh, slow down there Ken,' Gramps said. 'It says you have to be 16 or over, so you've a few more years to go yet, I'm sorry to say.'

I was disappointed but at least mum said she would try to get one, and Gramps agreed to take the form in with his next time he went over to the council offices and get them both authorised together.

'I believe they made a few announcements on the wireless about the tests, have you picked up anything as a broadcast?' asked Gramps.

'No,' said mum, 'we've not had much chance to listen to the wireless recently.' They had been rather busy on the farm and Michael was now getting in on the act as he'd try to tune in and listen to the cricket scores.

'You know how he loves his cricket,' she said. 'And I'm regularly being updated on the major games. He tells all the locals at The Plough when he goes in, for a pint. His friend Geoffrey has dropped in twice in the last week, and I'm sure it's only to see how the crickets progressing. We would only ever see him once in a blue moon before that. I am thinking of posting a notice on the back door when England are playing all India at the Oval in August with the latest lunch time scores. So, if you see a trail of visitors, you'll know what they are up to.'

Gramps laughed and said, 'That'll teach you to be so popular,' and then asked how I was getting on with the scrapbook.

You must have made some sort of a start by now with what we had from the Grand Prix, but have you been able to add any more bits and pieces?' Gramps enquired.

Chapter 11: Scrapbook

I then told him about my visits with Tom and how I helped him by running errands for him while I was over there. Sometimes I told him I even got to take messages from the telephone operator to some of the drivers or carried messages from one Marshalls point to another.

'I'm getting to know the place like the back of my hand,' I said trying to sound casual.

'Why don't you go and get the book Ken?' said Mum. Then you and Gramps can sit in the snug and have a good look at it. 'I'll bring you in a cup of tea pops,' she continued, 'You are looking a little tired.' (Pops was a pet name she used for Gramps on occasion).

To be allowed in the snug in the daytime, I couldn't remember when that happened before. The best room in the house was like a cosy den and normally reserved for evenings, after a hard day's work as Dad put it. The curtains would be drawn and the smoke from the fireplace danced with the flames and swept up the chimney. Then mum would light the oil lamps and I'd never get long in there as it was always my bedtime at just after seven. Now as we went in the light filtered into the room through the long sash windows and the cushions of the chintz settee seemed to engulf you when you sat in them. Mum had just spent weeks recovering them and it had added a lovely fresh appearance to the room.

While Gramps went to have another look at the picture of me sitting in the Alfa Romeo, I dashed off to get the scrap book. He was still admiring the picture in its new frame that mum had got from the jewellery shop in Loughborough. It was in a silver frame which I'd had to polish a few days before, so it still retained its lustre. I nudged him with the book and then he turned.

'My that was quick,' he said. 'Can you always run that fast? I've hardly had time to look at the photograph, and I do like the frame that was emblazoned with egg and dart moulding around its perimeter. It is considered very fashionable at the moment I believe. Your mum's made a good choice there,' he said. 'A bit like her mother in that respect, although you were too young to remember your grand—mother, she died when you were about a year old.'

'I don't remember that far back!' I said. 'But I'm sure if she was as nice as you, I'd miss her heaps.'

'She would be right proud of you our Ken, to hear you speaking like that, and she would want to see your scrap book also.'

With that he took it out of my hands, and we sat together on the settee. He seemed so absorbed in it for a while and everything went so quiet that I could hear the clock ticking on the mantlepiece When he looked up, he smiled, blue eyes set in a slightly weathered face and a crop of unruly brown hair that was just beginning to tinge with silver that never seemed to sit down on his head.

'You have been busy,' he said. 'You've done really well. It's certainly proved to have some perks being able to go with Tom and help him on the marshalling posts and running errands. Just make sure you don't get in anyone's way over there.'

'Oh no gramps, all the drivers and mechanics are so friendly and I've even started writing to one of them and he said he would send me some postcards when he travels abroad, to race. His name's Raymond Mayes and he says he travels all over the continent now, but it makes it hard just to cheer for one person when you want them all to win.'

Gramps laughed and then Mum came to join us.

'What do you think?' said mum.

'He seems to be doing really well with this scrap-book,' said gramps. 'You must have spent a lot of time on it Ken.'
'Look at this,' he pointed out to mum. 'There's even some pit times for some drivers and you have loads of passes.'

I then told him I found it really interesting and had often watched the mechanics change the tyres and check the oil gauge.

'I'll be able to do yours for you gramps,' I said.

'Not just at the moment our Ken,' he said. 'But in a few years' time when you are a bit bigger you'll be a useful guy to have around if you can work on motor cars.'

'How is the Bugatti going now?' he asked mum.

'It's good,' she said, 'and I enjoy driving it.'

Gramps continued, 'What I thought that I would do is leave the saloon here with you and Michael and then I could take the car down for some trialling with the Midland Automobile Club. It would mean I have to take John with me. He is proving to be very good on the maintenance, since that meeting with Jenkins earlier in the year.'

'Jenkins?' said Mum.

'The mechanic of Martins who came over to the farm,' Gramps said.
'Oh, yes,' said mum, 'but will it be safe?'

'Of course,' said Gramps. 'It's a marvellous opportunity and will possibly give me an insight into this racing business.'

'Can I come Gramps?' I asked.

'Afraid not,' said Gramps. 'It will be my first visit and from what I've heard of the rules you're not allowed more than two people in the car during trials and I would not want to lose you. Tell you what I will keep all the tickets and information and you can add then to the scrap book when I get back. By the way do you ever see anything of the young Italian boy 'E' that I dropped off I believe he lives locally now.'

'Oh yes Gramps, he is in my class at school, and sometimes comes over to play with my car collection. We are going to design a space for them to drive on. Thanks Gramps he's great.'

'Take good care of the cars Ken, they aren't so easy to come by now.'

Then he looked at mum and said he would like to bring more children over, 'If you and Michael could cope.'

'I'm sure we can,' said mum. 'As long as it's all legally sorted. You know what Michael's like.'

'I'm glad you said that,' said Gramps, 'there's a queue waiting to come across from Germany.'

I hoped that they would all be as nice as 'E' and was about to ask when mum changed the subject and said she'd like my help with the harvest this year.

'Can't have you shut upstairs all day, can we? You are old enough now to go with some of the other children in the fields, and you can always help with carrying up some of the drinks at lunchtime. Your Dad's already organised for the regular families to come over to work. Don't forget we've got to go and get some new winter clothes for you. You've shot up that much this year that your old jacket is halfway up your arms. Perhaps he's going to take after our side of family,' she said.

'Well, I think it's got more to do with all the good food you tuck into him,' said Gramps.

When the subject turned to food mum looked up with a start and said it was high time she got the tea on and was he staying. This time he was able to, but it seemed he was always so busy these days, that in no time he was leaving us again.

Mum and I did go to Loughborough to get some new clothes for me, and some bits for mum as Gramps had given mum the money, so we had quite a day out. It was always the same though my clothes always seemed to be a bit bigger than I needed 'so that I could have plenty of growing room' so mum said. Even my old ones I found out later were washed and put in a bag for one of the regular families that came for the harvest. They were for the Twelves and there was seven of them who came, and mum said it was a big family to feed and clothe.

It was a good summer that year and the cattle grazed lazily on the rich pastureland. Mum made packs of cheese and butter for the market. Dad was also pleased for a change as he said the hay had enough sunshine and just enough rain to produce a really high yield. Though we'd all have to pray for a good spell to gather it in. I can't say that he was really a religious man but
the good book as he called it was always kept in the drawer of the Welsh dresser and births deaths and marriages duly recorded. Passed down from his mother and his grandmother before him.

Whether or not the man upstairs was listening to him, I don't know, but he got his wish, and it was one of the best years ever. Dad had recruited the village people to help with the potato crop and gather the hay which we grew for winter feed for the cattle. They were the regulars who came from miles around every year. I remember them now the Betses, the Stop's, the Twelves, whole families. We'd work from morning to dusk and even a good harvest moon if there was one. No one wasted a second and mum would take them up drinks in the fields.

Wilf and Harry the shires were kept busy carting a lot of the hay down to the long barn where it was then stacked for the winter. Afterwards everyone would be invited for the harvest supper and we'd draw up the trestle tables and long benches. Some of the girls would make corn dollies for decoration and mum seemed to bake all day This was a good year so she made a huge hot steak and kidney pudding followed by apple cake with lashings of hot custard. Dad organised a couple of draught beer barrels from the local brewers for the party and it was a real good shindig. Mike Dalby brought his harmonica over to provide the music and we all partied late into the night. The lanterns had been lit and no one wanted to go home.

My friend Jeffrey and I had homemade lemonade with the rest of the children, but he managed to find a half empty glass of beer which we emptied into our own glasses. I don't think anyone ever knew, but I did feel very woozy and giggly afterwards. It was a long time before I tried any alcoholic drink after that and I'm still not keen.

In no time at all it seemed that another term had started for school and there was no shirking. Dad was adamant that I should not end up just another farm hand, so even if I did feel ill I went to school because otherwise I was packed off up to bed all day which was dead boring, although I loved my room. It was
high in the top of house and set under the side pitch that seemed to come down at an angle on one side and if it rained hard enough I could hear the drops lashing down on the tiles outside. My brother Jack had his room on the other side as the house was symmetric in that respect. From the window I could see to the other side of the valley and to the tiny beck that burbled its way down from a small spring which fed the farm. It was reputed that the romans had some sort of site near the farmhouse and had drawn the water down from the spring through old clay pipes which Dad occasionally found in the fields, but most of them were beyond use once the shires had trodden on them. It was a good window to watch from and occasionally if I knew when Gramps was coming, I'd dash upstairs and see if I could spot him coming down the twisty lane that led to the farm.

I was due to go to the 1936 Grand Prix at Donington with Tom and had been excitedly talking about it to Mum. There would be some big names there and I had been reading the Motorsport magazine for updates. I was so disappointed though when I went down with measles and both mum and dad agreed that I was not to go anywhere and had to stay in my room. Tom came over much later and gave me his programme and said I had been missed by the Marshalls, but it didn't make up for the real event. Life didn't seem fair.

Chapter 12: Bugatti time trials

Gramps came over the weekend after his trials. He said that he had had a great experience but he'd take his hat off to any racing chap now.

'It's not as easy as you'd think,' he said, 'and would you believe it, after such a good summer, it had to rain, and there's no stopping even for the weather.'

The chaps at the Midland Automobile Club gave him a lot of tips and advice and had been extremely helpful, but they just couldn't organise the weather, could they and he laughed.

'So do tell us what happened,' said Mum, 'did you win?'

'Did I win? It's not as easy as that, in my case, it was could Jenkins and I get started? The course which is above Broadway is a little beaten up earth track that threads its way through the trees on the upper slopes of a place called Fish hill. The way its laid out it now officially gives the club two hills for trials,
and it's all so new that even some of the other entrants didn't know of the new layout. I had arrived early and put some extra petrol in at Broadway with the hope of having a good look around, but the sky became almost jet black and was just about beginning to spot. So, I was directed by some of the marshals to go along a narrow track amongst the ferns and then drop down a steep grassy bank to turn back on myself up the hill which they had marked as the course.'

I interrupted him then and said that I wished I could have been there, but he said it was just as well I wasn't as by the end of the day he and Jenkins had been soaked through, and they had only just made it up the hill. The chap behind got thoroughly stuck in the mud as the heavens had opened and water was just running in rivers down the track. He couldn't move and they had to get two shires which were on standby to pull him out of the mud. This operation took so long, and it ended up delaying the whole schedule so the Marshall in charge a man by the name of Bill Vincent called the event off.

'Was it as bad as that?' asked Mum.

'Well,' said Gramps, 'It's just not the done thing to have the hood raised, so Jenkins and I managed to jam our hats down over our heads to cover our faces, and we buttoned our coats up to the chin. It got so bad that the water trickled down my chest and pools of water kept forming in my lap. We were pretty fed up, so I asked the boys what the form was and they advised me to go over to the Plough at Cheltenham where we managed to get a room for the night. Luckily, we were able to dry our clothes out and get a good hot bath and come the evening the Sandbac boys threw a party. After dinner the provisional results of the trials were announced. Somehow we'd managed to come fourth.'

'That's brilliant,' said mum and I together, 'did you get a rosette?'

'No,' said Gramps, 'but I was so delighted by the result that I asked if I would still be eligible for the entry the next day as part of the day had been cancelled. Bill Vincent was delighted and asked me if I would like to stand in for the day as part of the team as one of the regular drivers had gone down with flue, and I would be a great help in the match trials. So of course, I said I would. Come the morning though Jenkins had to take a look at the car as it refused to start, and he spent a good half an hour drying out the plugs as the engine had taken a fair battering. However, we managed to get it going and I was so anxious to do well and not let the team down that I nearly had a major accident before I turned the first corner.'

Oh no! 'What happened?' asked mum.

'I just tried to flash around the bank and I struck the side of the hill with the near wheel so that I broke some of the spokes and only just managed to stay on course.'

'It must have been an anxious moment for you then,' said mum.

'It was a bit,' said Gramps 'but it makes you realise just how good and exact a driver you have to be to get anywhere. Anyway, the result was that it ruined my time, and I couldn't get enough speed up and sank in the Cold slad hill. The other trials man who we were matched against was driving a M.G. Magnette, quite a nippy little motor with good mudguards and two huge spots on the front, and boy could it climb. He just ploughed straight through leaving a gigantic wash behind him.'

'So, what happened, did someone push you out?' I asked.

'No Ken,' he replied, 'It was too wet for that, they had to get the Shire horses out again and they towed us to the top of the hill. I think it was the same for most of the boys that day, so the whole match was classed as a draw. It was so wet again that to be frank, I was just glad to get home. Which made me realise that if anything major did happen to the car then it would be difficult to get home, but it was a great experience.'

'Not only that,' said mum. 'You could have overturned so easily in that little Bugatti of yours as well as catching a death of cold.'

'Oh, I'll be alright said Gramps but don't go worrying about it as I don't think I'm going to be able to spare the time in future to go trialling. I will stick to watching at Donington with young Ken here as often as I can, as some of the wines I'm bringing in from France are proving quite popular with the London set.'

Chapter 13: Alterations on Farm

'It's a good little number to have at the moment but things are in a bad way for some of my friends in Germany with Hitler having occupied the Rhineland. It's beginning to affect some of my model toy shipments a little as the officials now want to get their nose into everything, and there's a lot of red tape and paperwork to do before anything is allowed out of the country,' said Gramps.
I think I may have mentioned it before in passing, but much more serious now.
'Is it as bad as that?' said mum.

'I'm afraid so,' said Gramps, 'so make sure you keep your cars safe, as it may be difficult to get much more stock in the future. Has there been much about Europe on the radio recently?'

Mum hastily explained that they'd not had much time to listen recently as they had been rather busy on the farm.

'Since the harvest we've decided to knock down the old brick outhouse and make some alterations here in the house so we can have an indoor closet. We've also managed to get some old bricks from the gardens of the manse and we're going to have a soak away which Michael is building at the moment and digging out. On top of all the ordinary day to day running of the farm we've not had much time for anything else.'

'That's a great idea,' said Gramps, 'I was wondering what was going on in the farmyard when I drove in. Are you going to put a bathroom in as well?'

'It has been thought of,' said mum, 'but Michael and I think it would just be a little too expensive at the moment. Although we are taking the pipes up to the top of the house and having a holding tank put in. This is so that in the future we could then put a bathroom in the back box room, which is like a dressing room to the big bedroom.'

'If it would be of help,' said Gramps, 'I'm having some alterations to my house that I'm buying in London and I'm having to take out my old bath. It's got queen Anne legs and made of cast iron.' I didn't realise that the sale for the house in London had gone through pops. Oh yes said Gramps and I managed to get it at a good price and he gave a dry chuckle.

Really, but that's 'wonderful said mum, 'but how would we get it up here? Imagine having a bathroom here?

'I don't think it would be a problem,' said Gramps, 'as I could send it up in the guards van of the midlands train and you could arrange to pick it up from Loughborough.'

'Do you really think you could?' said mum.

'Consider it done,' said Gramps, as mum rushed out the door to tell Dad all about it.

Gramps and I grinned at each other; it was always good to see mum in high spirits.

Chapter 14: Christmas 1937

The winter seemed to close in quite quickly after Gramps' trialling, and we had a lot of heavy rain, the sort that brings in the leaden skies and long dank mists that blot the sun from the skies; but it didn't stop Dad from digging out the soak away and getting the bathroom up and running. A lot of the work was inside fitting pipes to carry the water up and down to the bathroom as it was going to be called, and mum promised me I could have the first bath. The tub was so big that when I lay down my feet couldn't reach the end, so mum made me sit up.

Sometimes to save water Jack used to get in after me and once I'm sure that my cousin Alex got so mucky in the farmyard that mum had to bath him as well. He refused to believe that it was so long I couldn't touch the end, until he had a go. He seemed such a silly boy that I was glad he didn't come over to see us very often. I never said anything as it was his brother Tom who had become an official at the racing park in Donington who took me with him on his trips over there.

Sometimes I'd meet my friends who lived in Park Lane as they still used their gap tickets to get in the place, but quite often I was so busy helping Tom and the organisers that I only had a few minutes to stop and talk. We now covered both the venues, the motor car racing and the motorcycle events and there was some cracking good races. My favourite rider in the motor cycle events was Ginger woods who rode a big twin Vincent-H.R.D, and when I told him about Raymond Mayes giving me his old tickets and passes for my scrap book he said he would save me his old tickets as well. He managed to find some from the Isle of Man where he raced in the Manx TT. My scrap book was beginning to fill up and I was going to ask Gramps if I should get another book. That way I'd have one for the motor cars and one for the motorcycles.

Come Christmas things were pretty quiet in the house, school had broken up and Mum started to decorate the house, and had Burt bring in some holly and mistletoe. I then asked her why she did this and she said it was an ancient custom of the Druids who gather together to celebrate the turning of the sun at the day of the winter solstice. Over the years the mistletoe had then been incorporated for fun and laughter for couples to kiss under. Then she reminded me sternly of our Christmas traditions which represented the birth of Jesus born to be the Saviour of the world. I didn't truly understand all that she said but looked forward to the Christmas dinner that mum produced and the flaming Christmas pudding. I always hoped I would get the coin that was hidden in it, but this year my brother was the lucky one. It seemed to be over all too quickly, but I felt sure I heard someone tapping on the back door on New Year's Eve. When I asked Mum about it the next day, she remarked that I had keen ears but I was right! She said it was a very old Scottish tradition that a man should bring a piece of coal into the house 'first footing' she called it, and it represented peace prosperity and good will and luck, to all who lived in the house.

Then it was back to school, Gramps came occasionally to drop more children off and he and Dad spent some time talking about tractors, and Dad thought he might make a purchase early summer. Which he did.

Chapter 15: Revenge at the Village Show

I think Mum must have been quietly seething about the carrot incident for some time and told Dad she wasn't going to be planting any more carrots for the show, but it wasn't going to stop her attending. She had decided to change her tactics and told Dad she would take the Bugatti and was going to enter for the best display of summer flowers and treat herself to a new outfit for the event. Dad did agree but as there was a while to go, he soon put it to the back of his mind. Not Mum, because we soon went off to Loughborough for a day out and the organising of mum's new outfit. She had an excellent figure and the Lady in the shop wasted no time in taking her measurements and telling her she could easily be a model for any fashion house she wanted. She had smiled and thanked her, but declined, and asked when she could pick the items up. She had taken great care in choosing the fabrics. In about two weeks' time the milliner advised Mum who was in high spirits then and after her return visit whisked the items upstairs.

It wasn't until a week before the show that she asked Dad if she could borrow Burt for the day of the show. To wash the Bugatti down and polish it till it shone, and even I had a blazer and was told to shine my shoes. The day before she had been in the garden and cut some of the old roses that had such a wonderful perfume that seemed to hang in the air and arranged them in a lovely cut glass bowl that had been her mothers.

Come the day everything was ready and when she came down to the kitchen she looked every inch the lady, and Dad looked speechless. She gave him a twirl in her new costume and he managed to stutter, 'go for it then lass.'

Then in a moment we were off in the car with me clutching the bowl which was secured tightly in the basket. She did cause quite a stir at the grandeur of her appearance and duly presented her flowers for 'Best summer flower arrangement'. No one seemed to doubt the outcome and she was duly present with a certificate for Best Flower arrangement in show, and Best Exhibit in show and finally presented with the show cup. We had a great day and even had time to stop for a cream tea. I did hear later that Sam Johnson had been beaten for the first time (in many years) and the winner was a young man fairly new in the district, but we both felt very happy going home later on in the afternoon. She did ask me if she should attempt one of her fathers' handbrake turns into the barn, but hastily abandoned the idea when she saw Dad in the farmyard. He did welcome us back warmly and smiled when he saw the show cup.

When he finally bought his tractor he seemed really pleased with the it and wanted to drive it around the farm anywhere he could. Apparently, it took some getting used to with all the pedals involved. True to his word though the shires were duly retired, and old Burt went to feed them first thing in the morning down by the Beck and took some carrots, essential to keep them happy. Even Mum was happy to see Dad driving.

'Even if it was only a tractor,' she said.

Somehow as the months passed Dad started to change and he became quite grumpy. Things started to get serious when Jack came in one day and complained to mum that he'd just about had enough of it! Mum was surprised and asked him what it was he'd had enough of?

'Well,' he replied, 'it's Dad he's always so grumpy these days and he often picks on me, just for the smallest of things.'

Mum was concerned and Jack then went on to say that if there was a war on he'd enlist straight away.

'Though I suppose you'll take his side,' he grumbled to mum.

Mum immediately said it wasn't fair to say such things as she knew her Michael was a fair man but promised Jack she'd keep an eye on the situation. Nothing much was said after that, but I noticed that Dad had become quite cutting to some of the farm workers and they now only spoke to him when they had to. I don't know how much longer things could go on, but Dad came in one morning in the summer holidays and suddenly snapped at me for being indoors. Mum had just come in from the back room then and stopped in her tracks. Then she came to the table where he had just sat down.

'Now Michael,' she said. 'I've got some words to say to you and I won't mince them. For the past few months, you've become quite grumpy, and nit picking and don't think others haven't noticed. Your own son Jack's complained and said he's ready to enlist if a war comes. Is it all the children gramps brings back, are they too much for you?'

'No,' he said quite surlily.

'What is it then?' she said, 'because if you are not more polite, I'm up and off and taking our Ken with me to live with Pops,' and she turned to go taking me with her.

Muttering, 'just when I thought things were looking up for everyone on the farm.'

Dad jumped up from the kitchen chair then or tried to as he shouted out 'No!' and nearly crashed to the floor.

'Michael?' she gasped, 'what is it, what's happening?'

'Oh lass,' he said almost in a whisper. 'It's my leg.'

It all came out then. Apparently, his gammy leg as he put it {it had never set properly when he had broken it as a young boy} was constantly playing up with him having to use it on the pedals of the tractor.

'Oh Michael,' she said almost in tears, 'that explains so much. Look let me think about this, I'm sure we can work things out. Battle plans and action stations! There was me even thinking you might have found a new lady at the pub,' and together they both laughed. I crept away after that.

Changes, when mum made her mind up about things that was it. Mum said they should buy some of the adjoining farmland with the old workers cottages on it.

'I did hear you say Michael that Mr Samuel would give you first option on it,' Mum said.

'Well,' said Michael, 'won't that mean even more work?'

'Not really,' said Mum, 'because you could ask Jack to take on more responsibilities and we could help him do up the cottages for him to live in.'

'Do you think it would work?' Dad asked.

'Yes, I think it would because you could then become more of a director of operations. Get old Burt to trim the orchard over there as well, you never know what's going to happen in the next few years, going on what Pops says about Germany. We may be very pleased to be able to do this, and let's hope his wines are still proving popular.'

It was all agreed as planned, and Dad soon became like his old self, and he and Jack both became enthusiastic about the idea. Jack took to driving the tractor.

Chapter 16: Tourist Trophy

It was early August that Tom came over to say that there was going to be a new event on at the Park and it was going to be called the R.A.C International Tourist Trophy Race to be held on the 4th of September. He wanted to know if I would like to go there, to all four days of the event.

'Four days,' I said, 'how come?'

'Well apparently the owners had agreed to make changes to the track and lengthen it,' he said, 'so that they were eligible to run it. The track has now been lengthened to three and half miles, so I thought I'd go and see it.'

'Really,' I said.

'Oh, and I've heard Prince Bira will be there.' Then he slapped me on the shoulder and called me 'the lad.'

'Well, I'll have to ask Dad,' I said, 'if it's for four days.'

Luckily, he said yes, and when I told Gramps about it, it was his turn to be disappointed. And he said maybe there will be other times. Then he tried to laugh it off!

'You know me, lots of children to bring back, lots of wines and hopefully more toys to distribute and a London house to sort out.' Yet I knew in my heart that he loved motor cars just as much as I did.

Mum turned out to be a great help and volunteered to make sandwiches so that we could take them with us to the Park but even so I came back ravenously hungry at supper time. The first day I had been able to get good details of the alterations that they had made to the track, and it now looked very impressive and a lot longer to walk around. Come the second day I thought I could relax a little but because more cars were at the Park I was asked to carry more messages to the entrants. That's when it became more exciting for me because I could get to talk to some of the drivers and sometimes watch the mechanics working on the engines. Just near enough to see what they were doing but out of their way. I told Mum about it and mum was pleased to see that I was developing interests outside the farm as she put it.

Come the Friday they held the scrutineering for the cars and Tom and I were quite busy on duty helping and directing the drivers. When I took a programme home to show mum, she seemed just as interested in it as I was. The prize for the winning car was £500 and £300 for the person who finished second, and even a purse for third and fourth places. The programme was a minefield of information giving in-depth commentary of the drivers and the marques they represented. There was the foreign challenge of the French cars one entered by Louis Chiron who had recently won in a Talbot at the French Grand Prix and Rene Carriere in a Delahaye. The Germans had also put in a strong entry and there were four Frazer Nash B.M.W.'s. Even some of the Italians had come over in Simca-Fiats which were of Franco-Italian origin. Then of course there were our own British contenders with Dobson in an Austin, Wisdom in a Singer and Maclure in a Riley. She jokingly said she wished she could see it, especially as there was a woman driver who had entered, but wistfully held herself in check because there was just so much going on at the moment.

Come the day of the race Tom and I made a slightly earlier start than usual, and Mum called out, 'hold on tight!' as we left the farmyard.

It was a running start in those days with drivers jockeying for position throughout the race and I linked up with Tom to watch it.

What a race it was, and so exciting on the new course. It seemed to take ages now for the drivers to complete a lap, but they all still jockeyed for position at the hair pin, and of course no one wanted to give way, but the tannoy gave a good commentary and eventually Raymond Mayes won in an E.R.A C Type. 80 laps in 3 hours 14 minutes and 29 seconds!

We stayed for the presentation of the trophies and by the time we left the park {there had been thousands of spectators there} it well past 6 o'clock. But I had even more memorabilia for my scrap book, and I couldn't wait to tell Gramps and Mum all about it!

We were both in high spirits going home but Tom asked me if I was still up for going to the 37 Grand Prix in a few weeks' time.

'Yes,' I said, 'that would be great.'

Tom said he'd pick me up same as usual.

'Yes please same time as usual!' I said.

Chapter 17: Confined to bed

I've been looking out for Information in the Motorsport magazine, and they are doing a great coverage now, as it was so popular and considered to be a top class International event. I noticed that Mum often took a look over my shoulder when I was reading the magazine.

I even counted the days down, only 5 days to go, but then we had a visitor to the farm. It was Tom's Dad to say that Tom had come down with a serious bout of influenza and would not be able to go anywhere. They had to get the Doctor out and he was confined to bed.

Talk about a disappointment, I wanted to kick the kitchen table, but one look at Dad's face told me that sort of behaviour wouldn't be tolerated.

I then asked if he could take me, but all he said was that there would be other Grand Prix's to go to.

'Could Old Burt take me?' I asked desperately.

'No,' said Dad quite adamantly, 'and if you think you can get your mother to take you, the answer would still be no, and certainly not in that Bugatti of your grand-fathers.'

I must say even Mum looked a bit disappointed then.

'It's my final decision Ken. I'm afraid you will just have to get used to it ken. Take it on the chin,' and he walked out of the kitchen.

I knew then that it was no use pleading with him, as once he had made up his mind that was it. Tom told me later he had been bitterly disappointed as well but had felt so ill he was just glad to stay in bed. Then he produced a surprise a programme of the Grand Prix with a few signatures in it which one of the organisers had given to him with instructions to pass it on to 'the lad'.

'Never gave me one,' he grumbled half-jokingly.

It was a bittersweet pill, but Tom said we'd go next year for sure and he ruffled my hair. I told him then if he wasn't careful, he'd be competing with Gramps as the best present giver ever.

It was a long time before I started to put things in perspective, and it wasn't until Gramps next visit, he told me just how lucky I had been to be able to go the R.A.C. International Tourist Trophy Race, that I jolted to my senses.

'Four days!' he said in awe, 'there's not many a young lad who would be fortunate to go for just one day, let along four!'

It was then that I showed him the programme for the '37 Grand Prix.

'Just where did you get this?' he asked.

I explained that the organisers had sent it via Tom, saying they missed 'the lad'. Gramps looked at it and then said thoughtfully that I must be a big help to them and he was sure they must think very highly of me.

'I'm really proud of you our Ken, really proud,' praise indeed from Gramps.

I glowed, and even Dad asked to see the programme later on. Gramps stayed on for a few days and spent some time talking with Dad.

It seemed to be a good year for mum this year because Gramps brought her a present when he returned to the farm to drop some more children off, and he was pleased to hear all about the results of the show, although I thought she had told him already!

We were in the kitchen when he gave her his present. She gave a gasp when she had peeled off the wrapping. It was a lovely statue of a beautifully sculptured lady leaning slightly forward, like a fairy with wings. Mum was thrilled with it and hugged him so tightly.

'You're the best present giver ever,' she said, 'and just where did you find this?' she said.

At first Gramps wasn't keen to tell her but eventually he did. He said he had been contacted by a young Jewish sculptor who had managed to get a travel permit from the Foreign office in Berlin. He had been advised by the man to take a few of his pieces with him. Apparently, he had then been able to track me down through a Jewish connection in the area. He implored me to give him a lift to the border if I could, as he really wanted to find his way to Sweden. Naturally, I was reluctant at first and I explained that I only took children, but he seemed so desperate that I agreed and made him sit up the front with me. It actually worked quite well and before I finally dropped him off, he gave me a sculpture and said it marked his way to freedom. I don't know who was more grateful, he or I. It was such a beautiful gift. Mum was silent for a moment and seemed to be quite emotional and then said she would put it on the mantelpiece and named it 'The Flight to Freedom', and it stayed there.

Pace at the farm really picked up the year of '38 with Gramps dropping off more and more children. It seemed that no sooner had one group left than another one was arriving. Sometimes they left a little vase, or a small figurine. The mantelpiece was filling up with presents for Mum. I tried my best to quell the fears of small, worried faces and once one of the boys tried to tell me he was grateful for a good meal and the steady order that seemed to pervade the house that kept him going.

'No hiding in cupboards!' he said. As he almost shrunk back into himself and looked over his shoulder.

Chapter 18: Dunlop come to the Park

The next big event at the track that Tom kept me informed about was the Dunlop Jubilee and boy did I want to go! This was a brand new event and organised by the Dunlop tyre company. Quite different from one of the normal events as it celebrated the history of the tyre which Dunlop marketed, and they had chosen Donington Park as their venue. This sounded too exciting to miss and of course I said yes, and we arranged to meet early and Mum provided the sandwiches.

The Park seemed to have a festive air about it when Tom and I arrived. He always liked to be early and took his marshalling very seriously, but I was keen after checking in, to be up and off to have a good look around. One of the first things that caught my eye and made me curious was seeing a man checking the tyre pressures on a motorbike. So, I asked him about it. And he replied that tyre pressures were so important on any vehicles and that he was from Dunlop and they had been making tyres now for a long time and wanted to go on improving their development.

Then he grumbled and went on to say, 'The young riders of today just don't realise how lucky they are to have tyres that will last a whole race. Do you know that up until the late 20's riders would often carry a spare tyre on their backs specially in the Isle of Man TT. Races as the tyres then weren't guaranteed to last the distance?' I did wonder fleetingly then how often Tom checked his tyres, but we had always arrived safely so I put it to the back of my mind.

There was a lovely festive air about the place as the Dunlop Works Band played some popular tunes of the day and I thought how mum and dad might have liked to have heard 'Me and my girl'. Quite a few of the famous riders attended and I was quite lucky I managed to get Stanley Wood's autograph and E.R. Thomas's and quite a few more. Later on that afternoon there was a record attempt by Norton Motors to break the lap record. It was so exciting, and I heard it on the commentary box.

I was kept so busy that day running messages for people (and collecting autographs) I hardly had time to stop for lunch. Even Tom said he'd been busy with people asking questions about the racetrack, and where to watch. Then it was time to go. There was never another event like it, as it seemed such a festive occasion with the brass band, and the big marquee selling teas.

We were both weary by the time we headed for home. Tom just said hang on tight! One thing I always remembered from that day was to ask Gramps about the pressures on his tyres and Toms'. Gramps always joked and told me it wouldn't be long before I could check the pressures for him and (It wasn't long before I did).

It was nice getting home. Mum was always interested in what I'd been up to but even she was surprised at how many signatures I had collected that day.

'You will be needing another scrap book soon,' she said.

'It was a corking day mum,' I said, 'you'd have liked it if you and Dad had gone. The band played some really good tunes.'

Mum smiled and said, 'another time Ken another time.'

Tom had arranged to keep in touch and asked me if I was still up for the '38 Grand Prix.

'Same practise as usual,' he said,' pick you up and we can have an early start.'

'Yes,' I said, 'sure thing, I don't want to miss this event, not after missing out last year and the year before that!'

It was about a month later just after Harvest that Tom sent another message over saying the Grand Prix had been changed, and there was some confusion over the issue now. Everyone had been looking forward to the German contingent coming over to the race. Apparently, they had got across the channel and then been recalled for political reasons. In the end they were allowed by Hitler to come over to race as it was such a prestigious event. Fred Craner changed the date of the Grand Prix to October, which was more suitable for them, I heaved a sigh of relief when I heard this. At least they were still coming and the race had now been rescheduled for the 22nd October, which was during half term at school. I tried my best to get into everyone's good books and read every article in the Motorsport magazine to give me a low-down of who was racing. Oh boy this was going to be truly exciting. Dad advised me before I went and said not to get in anyone's way as he had heard there were going to be big crowds there, but I never told him they had over 60,000 people there that day.

'Yes Dad,' I said, 'but the marshals keep a good eye out for me and I am know as 'the lad''.

'Oh yes,' he said gruffly.

Come the day I was up early and down to the kitchen.

'Breakfast,' mum said, 'you will need something solid if you're running around that Park.'

I almost felt too excited to eat and had only just finished when Tom came into the yard. I quickly put my coat on, and Mum put the hamper in my hands, as I turned to go out the door.

'Have a good day,' she called.

Tom revved the motorcycle and I climbed on the back and we were off. It seemed to be busy even at this early time of day and the traffic soon came to a crawl, but Tom was good at weaving in and out. I just held on as tight as I could. With our passes, we soon parked up and Tom exchanged greetings with the marshal.

'Good to see you two here today, we are expecting large numbers, take care laddie he called to me. Oh, and take special care if you have to go around Coppice, heard Nuvolari hit a stag there in practise yesterday. Luckily, he's all right but he's badly bruised and heavily bandaged around the torso. Hasn't stopped him driving! Should be a good race.'

After our official check ins, I was off to have a good look around the pits. I had read in the Motorsport magazine that there was a strong contingent from abroad, the French had come over with the Delahyes, the Germans with the Auto Unions and the Mercedes Benz, and the British contenders were here with the E.R.A's, and I was keen to go and see them all. There was still plenty of time I reckoned, before I was due to collect any messages from the telephone booth to take to any of the drivers. It would be great to see Nuvolari and his car and I hoped I would come across him soon. It was as I was going along the pit lane that I realised the Auto Unions were nowhere to be seen, so I plucked up courage and tried to enquire casually where the Auto Unions were. I was then told that they were in one of the barns near The Hall and there was a guard on the door.

'No getting in there,' he said and laughed, but I was curious.

Then I had an idea, surely the guard had to go for lunch sometime, I would take a chance just to see them up close and go there at lunchtime. I was nervous as the time approached but as I drew nearer, I realised the Guard had gone to lunch. I nipped inside, the Auto Unions, shiny sleek and fast. I went right up close and held one of the steering wheels, could smell the leather and for a moment dreamed I was racing it.

Crunch, I was back to earth like a jolt, it was the guard striding back with his cap on his head and looking very officious. I decided to brave it out, stuck my hands in my pockets and went to walk out. He looked at me most sternly and I hoped he wouldn't ask any questions. But I made it out the

door in the fresh air and breathed a sigh of relief. For one brief moment I had touched the car, a memory to treasure. Then it was back to messages to be run and my role as the lad. I was kept busy almost to the start.
It was the usual racing start and it was so exciting watching them get away. The race was over 250 miles and this involved a total of 80 laps and lapping at over 85 miles per hour. This was going to be some race. The tension mounted as drivers came into the pits and the tannoy kept everyone up to the minute as to progress. Nuvolari won. The crowd was jubilant as it had been a gripping race and were slow to disperse. We all wanted to savour the moment. Tom and I met up later, and I climbed on the back of the bike, hung on tight and he took me home. I wanted to tell mum all about it when I went in, and I told her how exciting it had been.

'Some of the drivers think the tracks second to none, the best in Europe mum, and if all goes well they will have another one next year.'

It had been a fabulous year with the two big races and Tom and I had got to go to both of them and I was already looking forward to next year. Sadly, it was never on.

Chapter 19: Breakdown

Dad came into the house the following morning to ask me if there would be any more races this year.

'Not big events Dad,' I said.

Then I told him how interesting the Grand Prix had been and there wasn't another one due till next year.

'Well, that's a bit of good news, because I can well do without lorries breaking down outside on the road. I tell you, Jack and I ended up pushing it out the way and up to the top barn even had to get the shires out. It was that heavy.'

He sounded none too pleased about the whole episode. 'The driver said he'd come back for it later. Hope he doesn't leave it for too long. 'Could well do without that sort of breakdown happening outside in the lane. He really seemed quite cross about it still so I thought it best not to enquire about it. Leave it to another day!

After the Grand Prix, we only saw Gramps occasionally as he was so busy doing his runs as he put it, dropping more and more children off.

I had been meaning to try and catch mum on her own in the kitchen and ask her about Becky the little girl Gramps had brought over from Germany. She seemed so happy on the farm and had really taken a shine to old Burt and tried to follow him even after feeding the shires but the days slipped passed and Gramps arrived again with more children.

Mum took one look at him and said, 'you are looking tired Dad. At least stay the night, go and sit in the snug. I will make you a nice cup of tea with a wee dram in it,' she told him severely.

'You can't go on like this you know you need a good rest. You've done such a lot recently driving. Stay for a night or two? Then you can at least see our Kens track and layout he's been making. He and 'E' have spent ages on it, it is very impressive I can tell you now.'

'Oh lass,' he said, 'I'd love to stop longer but this time I have a deadline to meet.'

Mum came into the snug to talk with him then.

'Deadline what sort of deadline are you talking about Dad?'

'Well, I have been asked by the chap in the foreign office, you know the one who issues the visas, to bring a whole family across this time.'

'A whole family did I hear you say?' Mum asked.

'Yes. The father was a top neurosurgeon, a German Jew who has been banned by the Germans from practising. So, he was side lined and given a job working as a medical director in Breslau, his name's Ludwig Guttmann. It's really not safe in Germany anymore for Jewish people so Foley's asked me to bring him and his family back. He's even arranged a special pick-up point for him late at night, so I've got to be back in Germany for the 25th of this month.'

'Oh Dad,' she said, 'just stay the one night and then go early tomorrow.'

'Perhaps you're right,' he said, 'but I will have to make it very early and catch a later ferry.'

Then mum said a whole family would be very difficult to accommodate, but Gramps interrupted her then and said that apparently they had friends in Cambridge and he would be dropping them off there.

[I heard later that he went to Stoke Mandeville and treated some of the patients at the hospital there and went on to found the paralympic games.]

'That's good to hear, very good. Did I tell you about the visit we had from the local constabulary?' Mum said.

'No,' said Gramps,

'One of my husband's old school friends. Apparently, some-one reported us for trafficking children. Well luckily he was able to show him 'E''s old visa. You remember the very first lad you bought over, friend of our Ken's? He had left them here. The situation was cleared up very quickly, but he advised us to keep our activities to a low profile, as some people don't like Jews or German people. So, Michael left him with the assumption that anyone coming here has a visa from the foreign office.'

Gramps smiled then and said, 'Michael's a clever man lassie, a clever man.'

Then mum went on to say that she hoped that Becky would be safe for now, but we should still try and look for her family. Although as an after-thought she said the child would be a lot better off here than in Germany, and she's well cared for and loved.

Mum went on to say, 'She has certainly put a new spring in old Burt's step now, and he's even asked to be allowed to take her back to his home where he lives with his sister for tea. They live in the little cottage called Meadow View. Even our Jack has time for her at the cottage he's doing up.'

'What sort of progress is he making there now?' asked Gramps.

'Oh, he has got some big ideas,' said mum, 'but he's also working very hard. He asked Michael if he can put a fairly large extension on the property and a large conservatory which would be south facing so I'm told. He seems to have so much more energy and enthusiasm for things these days, he's a changed man and everyone on the farm is supporting him. His father has told him that he did not think that there would be a problem with the planning as he knew just about everyone in that department, and as it was for a working farm, should go through easily. We all seem to be so busy these days,' and she sighed.

Then she glanced at me and said supper and bed.

'I've left Gerty one of the kitchen girls to see to the new arrivals, she's very good with children having been one of 7 in her family. She will find you something if you are still hungry!'

Then she turned to Gramps and said, 'do you think there will be a war coming?'

Gramps replied that everything was in a very serious state at the moment and he had recently spoken to an acquaintance in London who said he was very apprehensive about his daughter Mary who had recently gone to France for a four week study course in Paris to brush up on her languages, French, German, Italian and Spanish. She had been told by the British consulate that they were going to be recalled early and were advised they would be back by the 28th. He said he was going to meet her at Victoria Station.

'Oh Pops,' Mum said, 'are you sure it's safe for you to still go over? After all you've worked so hard already.'

'Now don't worry lass it will probably be my last trip and I'm pretty confident about getting past the check-points and they all have papers. And I always leave a couple of good bottles of cognac in the boot for border control which they seem rather partial to. So I should be back in England by the 28th, if not before. And how about another cup of tea rather like the last one you made?' he said as he quickly changed the subject.

It turned out he was right; it was his final trip to Germany before the war broke out.

Mum was a bit edgy for the following few days and every time she thought she heard someone come into the drive she would look to see who it was. True to his word Gramps did arrive back just after the 28th with some more children that he had brought over with him when he had brought the German family over. He said that he didn't have the heart to turn them away when there were a few empty seats. Apparently, he told mum that Foley had actually hidden them at his own house, at great risk. Mum was nearly in tears but she gave him a big hug.

'Glad you are back, so glad.'

'Foleys put himself at great risk too and even he said he was going to leave. I offered him a lift but he refused and said he still had some things to do. There were troops everywhere. I do hope that young girl Mary got back from France alright, but her father as I recall said she was going to catch a boat from Calais to Dover,' Gramps said.

He then changed the subject and asked me what I had been up to recently and I told him then about the plans 'E' and I had. That we were working hard on the track in the attic for the model cars.

'I'll show you when its finished Gramps,' I said excitedly.

'Take your time and do it well our Ken,' he said.

Chapter 20: New Land

It took 'E' and I quite a while to build the track for the cars, but it was really worth it in the end. Dad even queried what we were doing in the attic on a warm day, but he was impressed when he and Gramps came to see it. They both stayed some time while we explained how we had made it and told them about the cars and the engines. We had spent hours with bits of paper-mache and paints, trying to get the layout correct.

Even Jack seemed to look at me with a newfound respect, as I overheard him telling mum that he always thought I had been a bit spoilt by Gramps and just been going on trips to the Park so that I could brag about it.

'Perhaps he has learnt something after all,' he said wryly.

'Oh believe me Jack he's not been idle,' said Mum. 'He's knows how to barter, and one day he will be able to do the mechanics on Gramps cars, or even yours if you get one, as he has been watching them quite closely.at the Park when they inspect their motors for the races, I've been told. He's really enthusiastic about it all and after all one day he has to make his own way and earn his own living. So don't be harsh on the lad.'

Jack was thoughtful and then said he had no idea he has such a good head on his shoulders.

Then mum asked him about the renovations, and he told her that she must come over and see the progress he had made.

'The new roofs on and we are just waiting for the planning permission for the new extension and the conservatory. We've had plans drawn up and the council sit this week. Old Burt has done some really good work around the place, he's even got a new least of life with Becky about. And he brings her over with one of the shires, Wilf and they go into the old orchard to work. He really dotes on her,' Jack said and mum nodded quietly.

Jack continued to say 'Oh and by the way I've negotiated a deal with the Shields family for some gravel from their quarry at Bredon for the track from the farmyard to the cottages so that it won't get too muddy. I've also ordered enough to cover the track down past the cottages that lead to the river.'

'I didn't realise that the land extended as far as that,' said Mum.

'Yes,' said Jack, 'we can even go fishing if anyone has the time. And I've even found a derelict barn down there. Better be off, work to do. Perhaps our Ken will turn out alright then after all,' and he walked off. 'See you soon!'

It was only a day or two later that mum had the radio on in the kitchen to listen to the news. It was grave, and she called for me to fetch Jack and my Dad into the kitchen. She told them then that there had been a special news bulletin and that King George VI had spoken to the nation. England were now at war with Germany. I think we were all stunned.

'War with Germany,' said Dad.

'Well, I thought it would come,' said Gramps.

'Really?' said Dad.

'Oh yes and there will be big changes and quite imminently I should think,' said Gramps.

Mum immediately turned to me and said, 'Don't you get any ideas about enlisting, you are far too young.'

Then Jack said, 'I think I should I'm the right age aren't I? it's a shame as I was really enjoying the work on the new acreage.'

So Gramps then said, 'I think we should all sit tight and let the authorities advise us, they will be around soon enough. The two German lads who were still with us awaiting their collection by their Grandfather became very distressed and asked Gramps if they were now going to be turned over to the authorities. Gramps hastily reassured them that nothing like that would happen and they were safe here. After all they did have their visas which had been issued by the foreign office. Even so they wanted to stay in the house and asked if they should hide in the cupboard despite reassurances from mum and dad, and were hugely relieved when their own Grandfather turned up to collect them.

Gramps then told mum that he was going back to his London house to see how alterations were progressing, and that he was having a telephone installed.

'I know there's a war on now, but I think at the moment it's where I need to be,' said Gramps.

'A telephone' said mum, 'and will it be safe for you down there?'

'Well its where my contacts are, and if I do get called up obviously I will let you know.'

'Oh Pops, everything is changing so quickly,' and she gave him a big hug.

'Oh, and it might be a good idea for you to have a telephone put in at the farm here then we could keep in contact much more easily,' said Gramps.

When Jack heard about the idea, he was very keen on it and thought it much more professional than writing letters and much better for business. I must say Dad was not so sure about the idea of the phone, but Jack persuaded him to at least look into the prospect and see about cost. It didn't take Jack very long to make the enquiries and they sent an engineer to come to the house and explain about the costs and setting a line up from the nearest link so that he could fit the telephone in the house. Dad then said that as the principle residence he thought that the phone should be at the farm, and Jack could make calls from it. The engineer then suggested that Jack could easily have an extension line put in when his house was completed at very little cost. As it was not far away. Mum was pleased as she said they would all be able to keep in touch with Gramps in London more easily, so he told us that it was lucky we had applied as he had so much more work on with the war, he only had a few spots left on his schedule to fit the work in. As it happened Gramps came up to see us a few days later, and I walked in on Gramps and Dad deep in conversation in the kitchen.

'Now you remember our Ken what goes on in this house stays in this house,' and I nodded. Then he said to me, 'you have been around this house, and the new build of Jacks, have you seen any nooks and crannies in the outlying areas where things could be stored?'

I thought for a moment and then looked at Gramps for help.

'Not really Dad. The only place that's dry and warm is the old shed set in the hillside where the shires are, and its right snug and warm there for them on a cold winters night. You aren't thinking of moving them?' I said hastily.

'No,' said Dad, 'and its wouldn't be big enough, but have you seen anything like that around Jack's new build?'

'Not really Dad, and I don't even think there's a cellar there either and I went with my friend 'E' for a good wander round the grounds only the other day when Jack was out.' I was curious by now and asked why he wanted to know.

'Well,' said Dad as he glanced at Gramps as though for approval.

'Well he's best told,' Gramps quickly interjected and went on to say that he had recently met with an old friend of his who was a curator at one of the museums in London and they were seeking quiet locations in the British Isles to store artifacts.

'Store artifacts?' I queried. 'But we are miles away from London, aren't we? Why?'

'Well,' continued Gramps, 'the gentleman in charge of the museums and the art galleries - I'm talking now about The Tate, and the British Museum do not believe it is going to be a safe place for items of antiquity to be stored in case the buildings get bombed. So they are transporting things out of the capital to safe locations. It's a very hush hush operation, and all the items need to be boxed up and stored in clean dry conditions with a guard at the door.'

'Really,' said Dad. 'I would like to help them,' he said 'but I think this is beyond us Gramps. After all we are only a rural farm and we've always relied on the farm dogs for our security.'

I think Gramps was disappointed then as Dad said we can't do everything, and Gramps laughed as he said, 'No Elgin Marbles for us, in the house!'

With Dad affirming – 'Not even the Elgin Marbles!

I did not think much more about it until we had a history lesson at school the following term and the teacher showed us a picture of the Elgin Marbles, but quickly remembered Dad's warning of what goes on in this house, stays in this house. I shut my mouth and stayed quiet.

Chapter 21: Telephone comes to the farm

Events happened quite quickly after that and an official from the army recruitment soon came knocking on the door. Jack was very keen to join up but was quickly turned down because of his flat feet, and Dad was told that as he had a Gammy leg he too was rejected. But the officer did say that as a working farm they were both needed to organise the day to day running of the place as several of the farm hands had enlisted. He even pointed out that he had been told that as Dad had recently acquired more acreage, he would definitely be needing Jack on hand as well. Dad grumbled then and asked how he was meant to keep the farm going with so few staff, but the Sergeant went on to say that if we were short of labour the army would send some prisons of war in to help or some land girls, and everyone must pull together to help with the war effort. Then Dad mentioned 'old Burt' but when they went to interview him, his birth certificate showed him to be over the age limit. Dad was quite pleased because as he told us later, at least he would have one good reliable worker other than Jack.

'Land girls,' he muttered, 'we haven't had women working in the fields before now. Good job it's coming on for winter I usually have to lay one or two of the men off anyway.'

Mum kept a tight hold of me in the kitchen saying to the sergeant that I was much too young to be going anywhere! And he nodded and agreed with mum. Dad was relieved to see them go and he pointed out quickly that at least he knew now, what the working arrangements on the farm would be. Jack was initially disappointed, but he soon perked up when he realised that he could really go ahead and make something of the new-build as he had begun to call it. It also transpired that Gramps was not eligible because of his age.

It didn't seem long after that, that we had a visit from Toms' dad (my friend who used to give me a lift to the motor racing track at Donington Park) and I wondered what he was doing here. He explained to Dad then that he had come over to see me and told Dad that his son had always thought well of me 'the lad' as I was known at the park. He wanted to give me a leaving gift, as he had enlisted in the army and had left on his motor bike only yesterday.

'What's this?' said Dad.

When I opened it, I was speechless, I just looked at him and the tears fell from my face.

'Now, now laddie,' he said pulling me into his arms, 'we'll miss him as well.'

As I explained to Dad later Jack must have been collecting his own memorabilia from the Park for quite some time as there were many names and signatures I didn't have. He later sent me a message to say that Tom had been sent to India motor bike and all.

Jack came into the kitchen one day and seemed quite downcast and told mum he had been disappointed with the army's decision and had received a white letter stuck on the door of the new-build. Mum told him not to worry about it then as she had just received a letter through the post from a relative in Tyneside. Their son had gone for an apprenticeship with Vickers engineering a couple of years ago and had shown such talent he had now been recruited onto the design team and was not permitted to join up either and he had received a white feather. It turned out later that he had helped on the design team for the D-Day landing crafts. Jack said it made him feel better knowing he was not the only person to be turned down and wasn't the only one to receive a white feather. I did not understand what a white feather meant so I asked mum, and she replied that some people just thought that if you did not enlist for the army, you were a coward, and sent a white feather as a symbol.

'Don't worry about it,' she said, 'our Jack's a good lad and I am sure he will be a lot more useful here with your Dad helping the war effort. By the way

I'm putting you in charge of the chickens, we will be needing as many eggs as possible!'

'Do I have to mum?'

'Yes, you do!' she said, and I knew then that I didn't have an option. Or I thought I didn't and neither did she.

The telephone engineer turned up a few days later and asked to see the 'gaffer'.

'It's about this telephone line,' he said to mum. 'You've asked for one to be installed, but where in the house are you going to be putting it have you thought about that?'

Dad came in then as he had seen the engineer driving into the farmyard and had gone across to ask Jack to come over. Jack was very pleased to see the man, and it was soon decided to have it installed in the kitchen with another line put in for the new build, as and when the property was finished.

'You were lucky,' said the engineer that I was able to book you in with the war conditions as they are. My schedule is booked up for weeks from now, it's all war work.'

Dad was a bit reluctant at first to have the second line put in until mum said she thought it was a good idea. So, it was settled and the engineer went to work.

Then he asked Dad if everyone who was going to use the phone knew how to use it properly? He said that it was quite easy once you knew how, and proceeded to unwrap a big black telephone, and said that it was made of Bakelite, that would be ours for the house and our number would be Loughborough 268.

'Now the knack is,' he said, 'lift the handle off the cradle and when you hear a burr sound on the line you can then dial the number you want, but please remember to let the central circle fall back to its original position before you start on the next number. How about the young lad having a go first?' he said to Dad.

Then he advised me to just speak clearly into the machine, 'there will be no need to shout, the person on the end of the line will be able to hear you quite clearly!'

I had two or three goes, of course I couldn't hear any one because he hadn't connected it! We all did, even mum.

'It will be connected by this afternoon just leave it to me,' he said.

Dad wondered who would be phoning us and Jack replied' 'as soon as you tell people that you have a number and think how easy it will be for you to contact the vet, and Gramps in London.'

Chapter 22: Resurrecting The Lorry

Within a week Dad was using the phone like an old hand, and I heard him say to mum that he wondered how we had managed without one.

The next day however I walked into the kitchen to see jack sitting at the desk cradling the phone and looking quite annoyed. It's all very well having a phone he muttered but it does help if people at the other end would answer it. Mum told him he would just have to be patient and who was he trying to contact?

'Well, it's your father in London,' he said, 'I want to ask him if his mechanic could come over sometime soon and try and get that old lorry fixed, it could be quite an asset.'

'What old lorry are you talking about?' I asked, 'and where is it?'

'Don't you remember?' said Jack, 'It was when one of your racing do's was on and traffic was everywhere, it caused us so much trouble. Your Dad and I helped push it out the way, and it has been stored in the top barn ever since. They didn't have time to fix it as they said they had a boat to catch. I can't think they would come back for it now and we could well make use of it!'

And he was so cross he said to me, 'If you know anything about engines you can fix it.'

I then pointed out to him with more bravado than I felt that I was sure I could if there were the tools to do the job with.

'Well, that's not a problem,' said Jack, 'there's a whole array of tools, set up almost like a workshop. Do you really think you can fix it Ken?'

'Well,' I said more cautiously. 'Now 'E' is coming over this afternoon we can certainly look at it.'

I was quite intrigued and then asked Jack what team it represented. But he replied that it must have been someone foreign because they had a ferry to catch. When 'E' came over I quickly told him about the lorry and he too was curious but said,

'Do you really think you can fix it Ken?'

'Well, I'm not sure I replied but I've seen lots of people working on engines and Gramps mechanic when he came over to look at his car at the farm taught me a lot about engines.'

'Okay,' 'E' said 'we can at least take a look. Let's go before Jack gets back, I don't want him breathing down my neck.'

It didn't take us long to walk up to the old barn and as we went inside I felt excited, who had the lorry belonged to?

'E' was thrilled, 'oh good it's got an instruction manual, and here are all the tools, and a handbook about the engine, that's great. I know my languages are a bit rusty but we can at least make a start.'

'Didn't realise you could read any foreign languages 'E',' I said.

'Well it was my grand-parents idea thought it might be good for me to acquire fluency skills in other languages and they both spoke in French and German when I went to visit them nearly every summer,' 'E' said.

'Let's get cracking then we can run through a check list first so we can identify what it is that needs fixing,' I said.

It was as we were checking the lorry that I realised that there was a huge storage compartment behind the main cab.

'Let's take a look at this' I said to 'E' excitedly.

But he said 'no let's wait and get this done first. Time for that later, your Jack might be here soon. And if you want to remain in his good books let's see if we can identify the problem.'

We had just finished the check list when Jack came in.

'I've been looking for you,' said Jack 'I was held up, but I see you have started without me.'

I wiped my oily hands on an old piece of cloth and tried to look impressionable and said, 'with 'E's help I have gone through the check list for the engine and we have been able to locate the problem.'

'Really,' said Jack, 'you serious?'

I then went on to say that as 'E' helped me to locate all the parts in the engine and we had been working hard ever since.

'Also we've found they carried lots of spare parts so I am hoping we won't have to send off for any replacements. I am confident that we can fix it for you Jack,' I said and 'E' agreed.

'Yes,' he said, 'sure thing.'

But as an afterthought I said if we need any leverage with a spanner or two we'll ask. So far we've managed though. Jack looked thoughtful and shook his head,

'Well Ken,' he said, 'I didn't think you two boys could pull it off, amazing. Can't wait to tell Dad,' he said. 'Can I leave you to finish off?'

'Hey wait a minute,' I said, 'you may have a problem because this is not an ordinary lorry,' and Jack groaned. 'I believe there may well be a car in the back. In the motor racing field this lorry is known as a transporter lorry and specially built for the job.'

'Oh, that won't be a problem,' said Jack. 'We can just off load it and leave it in the lean-to behind the barn. After all it's the lorry I want to use,' and he laughed and said 'I don't think they will be having any more do's at the Park for a while. If you two lads aren't doing anything you can help me shift it tomorrow, though I suppose we'll still have to store it, darn thing.'

'We'll help you shift it,' we both said in chorus as he sped down the track to speak to Dad.

'E' came back with me for supper later and mum said she had heard, 'that we had both been working hard at the old barn fixing the lorry,' she said with pride in her voice.

'You must both be hungry after all your hard work.' Then she said 'I hear there may well be an another car that was stored in the back, but what we'll do with it I don't know.'

'We can take care of it, we'll take care of it,' we both said in unison. 'We are going to help Jack shift it tomorrow and store it in the old barn.'

Mum looked at me keenly, but Dad then said, 'I hear you have been able to fix the old lorry boys. That's great news and it will be a great asset to us. You have really amazed me, Ken. Well done lads, well done.'

I explained then how 'E' had helped me, and he replied, 'great teamwork boys, great teamwork,' almost shaking his head in disbelief.

Chapter 23: Black Market Operations

It seemed that mum was in touch with Gramps in London, and he said he would be coming up to see us nearer Christmastime and she was looking forward to seeing him again as we all were.

It turned out he was going to be letting his home out in the village to a family he knew, a couple and their two children who lived in London. who felt they would be safer in a more rural environment.

'Well, I have given them first option, so I would like to go through it first and sort the house out,' said Gramps.

Mum was concerned then and asked him how long he was planning to stay and was it safe to go back?

There was a long discussion in the snug the night he arrived and even Jack sat in on things. Gramps said he'd heard people were desperate for supplies in the capital, and most of the food shops were empty as people had been trying to stock their larders. There was a talk of rationing of supplies and the issue of coupons so that everyone could have a share. Then he told Jack and Dad that already several of his friends had approached him to ask if he could get any extra supplies for them as they believed he had country-side connections. (They would pay good prices for them).

'Is it that bad down there now?' Dad asked.

'Yes,' Gramps replied.

'That's all very well,' said Dad 'but how would we get them down there. We can certainly increase the garden produce because I believe there must have been an excellent vegetable plot at the new acreage, but its fallow at the moment. We could put some more chickens up there and have more eggs.'

Then Gramps said, 'We could send them down on the overnight train to London and he could pick them up from Paddington. Milk, eggs, cheese, butter, pheasants, rabbits, this could be a very profitable business for us all Michael.'

'Yes,' said Dad 'but if you are talking of a fairly large quantity of food how often and when? I guess you've heard by now, our Ken and his pal 'E' have been able to fix that old lorry that had broken down that we had stored in the barn.'

'Well,' said Gramps, 'I had heard from Jack that you now had a lorry, and that the boys had fixed it, but where did it come from?'

'It was the one that was left here after one of them do's at the Park. We could transport the produce over to the station in that. When did you want to start though?' asked Dad.

'As soon as I get back to London,' said Gramps, 'and now you are on the phone I can liaise with you about the produce. What do you reckon?'

'Well, it's a big commitment but if you have the buyers for the produce we could go ahead as early as next week. We will have to increase output this end,' said Dad, 'get some more chickens, and churns for the milk.'

'Don't forget to send them back via the guards van. The chickens or the churns,' said Gramps as he laughed light heartedly and lifted the tension in the room.

'Don't forget our Ken,' said Dad, 'what goes on in this room stays in this room.'

'Yes Dad,' and I nodded at the same time.

It was after that I began to realise what an easy life I had enjoyed under the protection of mum's guidance and how enjoyable and informative my trips to the Park had been. I must say that life was never quite the same after that. {Gramps was right rationing was officially started on January 8th 1940 for butter sugar and bacon}.

The village constable came round a few days later to make enquiries about the new lorry that had been seen in the district and where did it come from? Jack soon told him it was a foreign one that had broken down outside the farm a couple of years ago. Fortunately for him 'E' had found the boarding passes for the lorry for its return voyage to Europe in the cab. Once he saw them he was quite satisfied and said an early acquisition of war spoils.

'Lucky man,' he said, 'a very lucky man. Make sure you register it with the ministry of transport. I want everything kept all ship-shape on my patch!' And he rode away on his bicycle.

Life picked up a pace after that and mum taught Edna how to churn the butter and make the cheeses. She was very good at doing this but as demand increased mum and Dad took on her sister Enid. Mum said they were both good workers, and this left Molly to do the main cooking.

It didn't take long for the planning permission for the extension to Jack's house to come through, and he seemed to be working on it day and night to get it finished.

Christmas had come and gone very quickly. Mum said it would be good to keep it traditional and everyone on the farm sat down to an excellent fayre, with Jack getting the coin. All too soon it was over with everyone back to work for the war effort. There were still cheeses to be made and cows to be milked. It had been an oasis of peace for just a brief time.

The days soon drew out and it was good to have the lighter evenings. Mum listened to the radio a lot more and told us that a man called Winston

Churchill had become Prime Minster, and he'd given a very rousing speech to the nation.

The sergeant came around shortly after that and asked Dad if he could join the Local Defence volunteers that he had been asked to organise. It was only once a week at the old village hall and there would be training in the defence of firearms. In the end it was agreed that Dad, Jack and old Burt were all eligible and duly signed up. Dad did say that he thought they had enough to do, but the sergeant pointed out there were very few eligible men about.

'I'm expecting to see you next Wednesday,' he said. '7.30 prompt. We should be finished by 10 o'clock.'

Everything went quite smoothly in the end and mum made sure that they all had an early supper.

One day Jack came into the kitchen saying he had just seen the postman who had given him a letter for mum which as far as he could tell was from somewhere foreign.

'Canada' said mum as she went to open it. 'Who do we know in Canada?' she said, 'that's writing to us.'

She soon found out. 'It's from your Gramps' side of the family, I believe they emigrated there after the Great War in the early 20's. It seems that a group of the boys have enlisted and are joining the war effort over here, and their mum is writing to ask if we could accommodate them if they have leave.'

'Really?' said Jack, 'who are they?'

'Part of the family are the Livermore's, Carl and Tex and also one of the Winter family boys, Charles Hugh Winters and they are leaving from pier 21 from Halifax Nova Scotia. I will see if I can contact Gramps and see if he can find out more, he's the man with all the contacts,' Mum said.

'I'm sure we could put them up in the new-build if they do turn up,' Jack offered.
'Jack that would be great and we could always feed them in the main house. You'll have to stop calling your house the new build though and think of a proper name for it you know' she chided him.

'All right, you think of one,' he challenged, 'it's a strange situation though as it's all part of the farm.'

Gramps soon put us all in the picture and said that a part of his side of the family had decided to emigrate after the Great war.

'They said they had had enough of fighting. Sold everything and boarded a ship for America. They were in such a hurry to get there that Tex was born on the boat as they were sailing.'

'Goodness gracious,' said mum, 'actually on board the boat?'

'Yes,' said Gramps, 'though we don't hear from them very often now. I believe they have done very well for themselves. You say they are coming over, when?'

'It doesn't give an exact date, but it would be good to see them as they are family.'

'Yes,' said Gramps. 'When the boys did come over, they said they had been given a lovely send off with a band playing on the pier from berth 21 from Halifax Nova Scotia. Their Dad had seen them aboard. They all joined the flying core, with Carl and Tex being navigator/bomber in Halifaxes and Charles became a tail gunner in a Lancaster.'

It was great to see them when they had time off, and they did say to mum how grateful they were as it felt as though they were coming to a safe haven. She always gave them plenty of food, a big hug when they went back to barracks, and sometimes they would leave me a bar of chocolate. Jack was always saying how helpful they were around the farm when they were on leave and looked forward to their visits.
'Come back soon,' he'd say.

Chapter 24: Dads Army

Mum was increasingly becoming quite concerned about Gramps being in London and liked to telephone him every day on some pretext or other. He told us all that it was quite safe because the sirens would start to wail and that meant that people should go down to their nearest tube station and sit on the platforms until the raid was over. These were well below ground level and people now used them all the time if they thought there was going to be a raid. Mum then asked if they had much warning and Gramps reassured her that watchers would contact the authorities in London if fighters were coming over the channel. He had been told that the Germans used Guildford Cathedral as a marker point for the turning point for London. Unfortunately the flight path later became known as 'bomb alley', but at least it gave the authorities time to turn the sirens on and alert people.

'Oh pops,' she said, 'just take care,' and gave him a wane smile.

'Listen lass they don't get it all their own way. Our lads are holding them off.'

Mum told him then about the Sergeant's visit and how Jack, Michael and Old Burt were now in the Local Defence volunteers and they went down to the village hall for drill every Wednesday and did he want to join them if he was up this way on a Wednesday? But Gramps said 'No,' as he thought the Sergeant might expect him to turn up every Wednesday, and there is too much to do at the moment, and his friends were so grateful for the food he could get, and did we think there was any way we could provide more. Dad was quite surprised and asked how much more as they had taken on two local girls to make more butter and cheeses.

'Well,' said Gramps, *'its whatever you can get hold of, and any fresh vegetables would be most welcome. I've heard the food queues can spill into the street outside the shops sometimes, and people will join one even*

if they don't know what they are queuing for. The rationing and the coupons are adequate but limited.
It was then that Dad brought up the identity of young Becky. 'Have you found anyone who knows anything of the child's identity?'

'At the moment,' said Mum, 'nobody knows of her existence only that she was dropped off with the other German children who had visas and it won't be long before she'll be of school age. She's no trouble here and Old Burt and his sister dote on her. Like a grandchild he never had, he told me the other day.'

Gramps shook his head then and said, 'I've made endless enquiries among the Jewish community but so far I've had no success at all.'

'I must say,' said mum 'she's thrived here and I wouldn't like to see her taken by the authorities and put into an orphanage ,and I can speak for all of us.'

Gramps was silent for a moment and then he said, 'I've heard that children are being evacuated out to the country from London so that they can escape from the bombings.'

'Oh,' said mum with raised hope in her voice, 'do you think we could say that she is one of those children? Say a child of a distant relative from London?'

'Yes,' said Gramps, 'I think that would solve the problem, and as I was the one to get us into this conundrum, I will be happy to pay for the child's upkeep. Do you think we can pull it off?'

Dad was thoughtful then and turned to me, 'You know the drill now Ken, what goes on in this house stays in this house. This is very serious do you understand?'

'Yes Dad,' and I nodded, 'yes Dad.'

We seemed to be constantly busy on the farm these days, but it wasn't long before the authorities came knocking on the door, 'an official visit to see mum and Dad,' so the lady said. She was quite officious in her manner and said that she was looking for rural housing which could accommodate evacuees, small children from London who would be safer here than living in an inner city. She then went on to say that perhaps mum could provide places? They would be arriving at Loughborough in two days' time. Mum said that she would be pleased to help but could only take one lad and went on to explain that she already had one young girl here who had come from London previously and was a relative of theirs.

'Becky her name is,' she said.

The woman looked at her then and said 'I hoped that you could take more.'

Mum explained it was a working farm with lots of cattle.

'If you are sure then,' she said, 'but can I rely on you to pick a young lad up from the contingent that's arriving on Thursday?'

Neither Jack or Dad were happy when they heard of the arrangement and said so. This is a working farm, but Mum then said that she really hadn't been given an option and that all rural communities were being asked to take children in. She then went on to say that we were lucky to be asked to take only one child in, as she had informed them that we had another child staying with us already.

'Okay, who's going to go and pick the child up then?'

It was agreed in the end that mum would go and take Gramps' old car the Bugatti.

'It will be good to give it a run out,' she said.

It seemed strange to have another child on the farm at first and he had seemed overawed the first few days. I think he must have been about 12 and he was nervous at first of the cattle, but he soon settled in and became a good friend, and a great help around the farm one way and another. He was very withdrawn though when anyone came to the farm as he was very conscious of a deep scar that ran down the side of his face. He was called Jacob.

When I asked him about it, he said he had been hit by a piece of masonry and the doctors had said they had patched it up the best they could and that he was lucky to be alive. Mum enrolled him in the local school. Later mum took a good look at the scar, and as it was still quite new, she produced an ointment for him and advised him to rub it on every day. One of the many jars she would make up in the summer. He never really liked school much and seemed happiest when he was with Jack or the shires or helping me with the egg collections.

It seemed that there was always something going on at the farm that had to be dealt with, we didn't have much time to listen to the radio. It was then we heard that clothing was going to be rationed, and I asked mum what would be next? She told me then, not to worry and said things would work out somehow.

Chapter 25: Mr. Fix It

By this time, we seemed to be sending more and more supplies down to London, and we now ran a few sheep on the new build, which mum and Dad now called the cottages. Jack took to going to the local the Kings Arms for a pint as he called it which sometimes turned into two or three. His sweetheart who he had been courting had left him after a couple of years and told him she wanted someone with more adventure and life. She had left the district and married an American GI, but It was when he was drinking at the pub that a travelling salesman approached him and asked him about his lorry.

'Fine bit of kit there,' he said. Then Jack told him that whenever it needed servicing his younger brother would do it for him. 'Makings of a real mechanic there,' he said. 'Real good Lad.'

'Well,' said the salesman. 'If he's that good, can he fix my Ford? Heard I've got to wait a few days before the garage can come out and fix it, and I'd counted on them to come out. What with this war on, time means money.'

'Well,' said Jack. 'I could ask him and his pal to take a look at your lorry if you like, no guarantees mind.'

As it was the weekend Jack drove us to take a look at it! Luckily, it was something quite simple. The man hadn't had it long and it hadn't been serviced for years but we soon got it going. It had always been a xxxx to start, and he gave Jack a bottle of Scotch Whiskey which Jack was well pleased with.

Dad was rather annoyed with Jack when he found out and said that he shouldn't be exploiting us as we were young boys. He said if we did things like that we should be properly rewarded. Though I could see he seemed really impressed.

As it turned out, Jack kept his bottle of scotch and produced it on his birthday at the Home guard meeting one Wednesday. As the Sergeant hadn't turned up Jack suggested they have a wee dram to celebrate and produced his bottle. All thoughts of training went out the window, so I was told afterwards and a couple of hours later with a good sing song the Sergeant came by to see if the village Hall had been locked up securely. Oh boy, he was livid and read them the riot act.

'Well inebriated!' he said.

Then he sacked them of all their duties and sent them shuffling home with heads hung low. It seemed strange in the morning as all the men were very quiet and seemed to be' tip toing' about the farm in a most low-key fashion. Mum even remarked that they were a bit late back last night and hoped the Sergeant wasn't working them too hard. It was a few days later when the Sergeant came by and asked mum if he could speak to Michael, Jack and Old Burt that mum found out. She had invited the Sergeant into the kitchen, so they all had to come in.

'Now,' he said, 'it's about your demotion, it would seem I cannot find anyone else eligible to replace any of you so, I've come around to reinstate you all to sign up for the Local Défense Volunteers.'

'What do you mean?' said mum. 'I thought they were all in the Volunteers already.'

Explanations and apologies soon followed but I could see mum was looking very cross. Dad stepped forward as their spokesperson and they all edged towards the door to try and get away quickly. Mum was having none of it and after the Sergeant advised them that he'd see them all again next week, she quickly slammed the door shut and rounded on them.

'You are all a disgrace to this household!' she said and told them all they had let the family down, and our good reputation and what sort of example were they setting for our young Ken here. She really gave them a good telling off. I didn't fancy being in Dad's shoes, and even I was glad to get out of the house later. She was muttering about it for days afterwards and told Gramps about it on the telephone. He tried to explain to her that it was tricky with the war being on and perhaps they had just 'let their hair down' and possibly things got a bit out of hand.

After that things slowly got back to normal, or as normal as they could be with a war on. Mum seemed to be listening more to the radio and she told Dad that things were getting a bit tough on the continent and the Germans seemed to be taking control of Europe. Churchill, according to Gramps was spending most of his time in London where there was a war office and he could plan the defences and was in contact with all the armed forces.

Dad sat the family down early one evening and told us that Churchill was a good man and we as a family were helping with the war effort and that was the best we could do.

'Everyone has to help out,' he told us and even Burt's sister was contributing and knitting socks to go in the parcels for the troops. 'We'll all pull together and we won't let anyone beat us,' he said. 'We are all lucky to be here and there's good food on the table for our meals, so let's all continue to work hard is that understood?' We all agreed.

Once the word got round that the boys could do a bit of fixing on the cars Dad took us aside and asked us if we wanted to carry on. We did, and by the end of the war we both had glowing reputations as Dad put it, and a handy bit of cash!

It didn't seem long after the home guard incident that Mum had a letter from another of Gramps relatives who lived on the south coast of England, and looked closely at the postmark.

'Dover' she said, 'who do we know in Dover?'

It turned out that it was a cousin who had two young boys and could she send them up for a break in their summer holidays as she believed we lived in a rural locality without any planes overhead. Mum contacted Gramps about it as she was initially reluctant to help.

'We've already got the new lad Jacob and young Becky,' she said.

Gramps then told her it was a rather unusual case and it was he who had advised her to write to Mum.

'Oh yes?' said mum frostily.

He went on to say that the two boys had been involved in the evacuation of Dunkirk.

'How?' said mum.

Apparently when they heard the call out for small boats to cross the channel and help with the evacuation, so they'd gone and taken it into their heads to commandeer the Vicars sailing dinghy which had a small motor attached.

'How they managed it, I just don't know but they joined the queue of boats out there and took off 6 soldiers who were standing in the water waiting, and brought them back home. How they achieved it with the boat so well overloaded was a miracle. But luckily, I was told the weather was as calm as a mill pond. They wanted to go back out again but were stopped as the weather had picked up a bit and not safe for such a tiny sailing dinghy like that. Really, they were just one of the many boats that went across, but to take it on at such a young age was quite remarkable. They are local heroes now but their mum's not happy as she thinks it has affected her younger sons' demeanour. He keeps on having nightmares and calls out in his sleep, so she was hoping a change of scenery would help them. The youngest is called Martin and the eldest is Malcolm. Can you help them lass?'

'Well,' said mum. 'I'll have to run it past Michael, but I should think we could squeeze them in, but they must understand it's a working farm and everyone pulls their weight here, even if it's only feeding the chickens and collecting the eggs.'

'Okay,' said Gramps. 'I knew you wouldn't let me down!'

Dad was reluctant but when he heard what they had done he agreed and advised that the young lad Jacob could show them the ropes.

'I don't think Jack will be happy but put it to him and see what he has to say,' Dad said.

It wasn't until later that evening at supper that mum said she had something important to tell us all and asked us to try and be understanding of the situation and told us what the two young boys had done. Jack was the first to speak and asked if mum really thought it would make a difference if they did come to stay? She pointed out that it would only be for the summer holidays.

'Where will they be housed?' he asked.

Mum said she thought perhaps in his house at the cottages.

'Well, it's not quite finished yet,' he said, 'and don't forget the airmen and Jacob has the only spare bed I've got.'

At this Jacob looked around very nervously at everyone as if he thought he would be asked to leave!

'Well,' said mum, 'we can soon rectify that. How about we get them some camp beds and perhaps they can share a room with Jacob? That way Jacob can show them the ropes and they could help around the farm. With

the increase in demand for more produce, they could be a great help. You could do that couldn't you Jacob?'
He gave a smile and said, 'yes mam.'

Jack thought about it and then said, 'I think you have this all worked out already mum,' and he gave a short laugh. 'We couldn't refuse them, could we? And if the weathers hot they may even like to camp out in the orchard,' as he warmed to the idea.

Chapter 26: Evacuees

Jacob told me later that he thought I had a great mum, as he thought for a while sitting at the table that he might have been asked to leave.

'No way Jacob you are part of the family now, mum won't let you down,' I said.

Then I found myself telling him that what goes on at the farm stays on the farm and he should not gossip about activities at school.

'You do understand what I'm trying to say don't you?'

'Oh yes,' he said my Grandfather in London was a bit enterprising and I knew when to keep my mouth shut. I was quite surprised as it was the first time I had ever heard him talk about his London life.

It didn't take long for Gramps to get things organised, and the next day he telephoned the house to say that the boys were on their way, and could Jack pick them up in his lorry from Loughborough? He explained to mum that he thought it would be better to use the lorry rather than the Bugatti as there was a lot more room. Mum then said it was a lot easier for her to go than Jack, as he was so busy on the farm. But Gramps said that he feared that there would be too much of a squash if she took the Bugatti no matter how small the boys were.

'Okay pops,' she said.

She then drove the lorry instead, after a few basic instructions from Jack. I don't think Dad was too pleased to see her driving the lorry, but all she said was that there was a war on, and she was only trying her best to help. It seemed strange when they sat down to supper that night. They seemed such small boys and I was itching to know all about them sailing the dinghy and how they managed it. Dad was telling them a bit about the farm and that Jacob could help them while they were here, but the youngest lad kept on looking at the ceiling and asked when the planes were likely to be coming over. Dad hastily reassured them that there were only a few, and that we were not on any direct flight paths. Jacob then spoke which was surprising as he hardly said a word and told Martin that he had lived in an inner city and the farm was like a peaceful haven in comparison. Even so he was a bit apprehensive. It did take them a while to settle. Martin told me all about his life on the coast later and said that he had learnt to sail in the Vicars' dinghy at a young age and had been in the choir. I told him then that I had never seen the sea and had only been on the river once when I was little. He then went on to say it seemed so easy just to take the vicar's dinghy because all we had to do was follow the trail of the other small boats crossing the channel.

'It was when we got there that we saw thousands of soldiers just waiting on the shore and some were in the water waiting for boats to take them to safety. With us being so small our dinghy could get almost into the shoreline and one of the soldiers helped some of his mates into the boat. We couldn't take him then, because we already had his mates. He waved them off then and told them he would catch the next sailing. We were well laden and just joined in the line of boats returning to Dover. I wanted to go back for him and I often wonder if he managed to come back. Once the authorities saw us when we entered harbour, they stopped us, and the soldiers were taken and sent on to some barracks, so I didn't see them again. Then they told us that we couldn't go out again in the dinghy as it had been a very risky thing to do and once the local paper got hold of it, we were considered heroes. They said it was a miracle that the water had been so calm. I just wanted to help,' he said, 'and I do hope the soldier's friend got taken off to safety,' and he became quiet again. I didn't know what to say, as I said to mum later, and she said that just by being there and listening would have helped enormously. We heard later that over 30,0000 troops had been taken off the beach at Dunkirk.

We were seeing a few planes flying overhead now and the next thing we heard was that Castle Donington airport was being seconded for the war effort and that military airplanes would be deployed there. Luckily for us we weren't under the direct flight path and Jack calculated we were southwest of it. I heard later that all the lovely old oak trees that were at coppice corner in the racing park had to be cut down so that they did not obstruct the flight path for the airmen landing and taking off. Off course there was the availability of extra firewood but mostly it was kept for the main hall, which was operating as a nursing home for injured service men.

It was a good summer that year and Jacob was an excellent help with the young boys and introduced them to Old Burt and Becky, and they seemed to gel into a tight knit community over there, and he took over the egg collecting and the chickens. This left me free to assist Jack more as the demand for the lad's 'doing some fixing' was growing, and even with 'E's' help I was often very tired at night. Mum was quite concerned and thought I should ease off a bit and perhaps go over to 'E's house out of the way of the farm and take off and go cycling for a day or two.

Far from going cycling though, we took the opportunity of going down to the barn where the old car was stored. What an opportunity it was! We stripped it down and just about took it apart and then put it back together again, and what a car it was! We had the steering wheel off in no time, and memories of the track came flooding back and all the good times. But Gramps phoned mum up early one morning which was usual as he normally only liaised with the farm about supplies now.

The news was grim and he said, 'the German bombers are coming in force over the channel and with their ferocity of their attack were trying to blitz the city of London every night. In the skies it was called the Battle of Britain and the Spitfire boys seemed to be constantly airborne fighting them off. With the Merlin engines they were a force to be reckoned with, swift, accurate and fast. I believe we will fight them off.'

He advised mum not to worry if she didn't hear from him daily, it would be because he was sheltering in the underground, but please continue with the supplies. Demand was continuing despite the troubled times.

All too soon it seemed to be harvest time and Dad had been keeping a close eye on the weather. It had been a good year and Dad said we should all be involved even if there was a war on as the hay had still to be gathered and stored for the winter. Our usual regulars came, and we worked from morning till night for several days, and the weather held and Mum organised the food for the harvest supper.

'A little respite from the war would do us good,' she said.
Christmas was quiet this year, Burt cut some holly and mistletoe for decorations, and I finally found the coin in the Christmas pudding.

Chapter 27: Rationing

Always at about this time of year mum would take me into Loughborough for my new winter clothes for school, and we'd spend a whole day browsing around the shops. But not this year, it was a quick in and out, and a visit to the girls' clothing department for Becky, not that she needed much because Burt's sister Ruth had been knitting thick winter jumpers, hats and mittens. It seemed she never stopped knitting and she soon set to and knitted jumpers for Jacob and myself. Fortunately, Gramps had been able to give mum a couple of old coats that he had stored in the house he was letting in the village and asked her if she could make use of them. Mum was delighted as the authorities had introduced clothes rationing.

Come the end of harvest Malcom asked mum if he could stay on the farm and pleaded with her saying he would be a good boy and not get in anyone's way. Mum asked him why and he said he felt safe here. It came out then that their mum always seemed to be dashing around doing war work since their Dad had joined the navy and didn't have much time to spend with the boys, and they often went to a neighbours after school. The end result was that they both stayed and mum enrolled them at the local school.

Mum took me aside one day in the summer holidays and she asked me to sit down at the kitchen table. I wondered what was coming next as the war was on, chickens to feed and cars to be mended.

She took me by surprise a bit, as she said, 'I know you are still a young lad Ken, but have you thought about your future and what you want to do? You could leave school next year and technically you could get an apprenticeship, or wait for a couple years, so let me know, and like it or not I believe you may have inherited flat feet like Jack so the forces wouldn't take you on.'

I was quite disappointed when she told me about my feet as I explained to her that a couple of the older boys at school had signed up and left the village. Perhaps I should do the same?
'Not if you have got flat feet Ken, not with flat feet,' she reiterated.

I asked her if I could think about it for a while, as it was difficult to make choices with a war still on. Then she said had 'E' any plans as he will have to decide as well? When I talked to 'E' about it later and broached the idea of going into a partnership to start a garage business with me, he told me then that if I wanted to set up a garage business, I would be more than capable of setting it up myself and running it.

'You are a natural engineer Ken,' he said, 'you seem able to take one look at a car and know how to fix it. All I want to do when this dam war is over, will be is to go back to Italy if I can, and live with my Grandfather where the weather is warmer and the skies sunnier.'

Then he went on to say that I should be careful what I chose, and did I really want to be fixing cars for the rest of my life? When I told mum later about my talk with 'E', she said 'he's right about what he's advised you. You still have some time, let us know. Choose wisely.'

It was after that I started to listen to the news more and heard that the Germans were now blitzing Coventry and the lovely old cathedral there had taken a direct hit and had almost been demolished.

I went to mum then and asked her, 'when will it all end ma. When?'

She replied that we all on the farm had to keep going and doing what we knew, keep the supplies going and believe that somehow, we'd win as a nation, and that Churchill would lead us to victory.

Initially I felt disappointed that 'E' was planning to go home as soon as the war ended, but he said that his heart wasn't here in England, and he disliked the cold damp weather and the lashing rains.

'You'll have to come and visit me when you're older,' he said. 'Do what you feel is best for you Ken and what makes you happy. You will have to spend a long time at work, until you retire,' and he laughed. 'Make sure you are doing a job you enjoy.'

That thought seemed to stay in my mind. Did I want to be running a garage business? Then I remembered the times I enjoyed best were when 'E' and I had been doing the design work for the track for the model cars, time had flown by then, and I had been truly absorbed in it but how was I going to get on a design team? I asked mum about it then, and I think she was initially surprised.

'You've got high ambitions Ken,' she said, 'but if you are serious I believe you can set your mind to achieving your goal, but it will mean some hard work.'

Then she went on to say, 'don't you remember one of our relatives in Tyneside went to Vickers Engineering and he went for an apprenticeship. The one who got a white feather! And was seconded to the design team?'

'Oh yes, but isn't that rather far away mum?'

'It would be but how about going for an apprenticeship at Rolls Royce in Derby? I believe your skills would be recognised and you could advance from there. A few of the local boys around here have done quite well for themselves there.'

'Do you really think so mum?' I said.

'Well, I've heard that they are keen to keep good apprentices on and offer them jobs, but with a recommendation from there you could go anywhere in the world when the war is over. If you wanted,' Mum said.

I decided then that was what I wanted to do but I still had a little time to go!

I think Dad and Jack were initially surprised at my decision to take on an apprenticeship at Derby and said that with my skills I should think about starting my own business. They hadn't reckoned with mum though as she was backing me, and said it was an opportunity that could lead to new beginnings and a good solid pay package at the end of it. Jack grumbled a bit and said I could always twist her around my little finger and she chided him and said, 'Now, now Jack, don't forget you stand to inherit this farm and young Ken has to make his own way in life.'

Chapter 28: Near Miss

Meanwhile the war seemed to carry on relentlessly and I was always busy after school. Mum insisted that we should all do our homework, as well as collecting the eggs, so we organised a rota with Malcolm and Martin so that one of us could do our homework first each day. Even so, I often felt tired and glad to get into bed at night.

With the onset of winter mum moved the two boys over to the main house where we used to house the Jewish children when they arrived, and she said it would be much warmer for them. The airmen when they came slept over with Jack at the cottages, but they all came over for a supper in the evening, and Molly was constantly cooking. We all seemed to share a sense of community by being there and it seemed that we always looked out for one another, and that the kitchen was a safe place to be and little Becky was the small girl we all looked after. The war seemed to roll on relentlessly.

Christmas came and for a brief moment again we stopped and had a traditional luncheon and Dad said we should cease our chatter for a moment. When it was quiet, he then asked the dear Lord to bless and keep safe all who were in this household and said how fortunate we were to have food on the table. Then he left to feed the cattle.

We did have one incident in the war when it was late at night when I heard a plane going low overhead. Dad said later that it must have been in trouble and found it had dropped a bomb in the field near where Wilf and Harry the shires had their stable set in the overhang of an old cave. He found it in the morning after we had all gone to school. It hadn't exploded and was sticking in the ground, so he called the army unit in to 'come and deal with it' as he put it and evacuated everyone to the cottages just to be on the safe side even the shires. When it was blown up it caused a bit of damage to the stables with the sheer force of the blast and fortunately was too far away to impact on the main house. Old Burt asked Dad if he could do the repairs as soon as possible. He loved the old shires, then it was back to work as normal. I think it gave us all a bit of a jolt though and made us think how well we had all fared up till now and how damaging bombs could be. All except one that is, Martin came in the kitchen to see mum the next morning and said he didn't feel safe here anymore and was frightened and didn't want to go to school anymore. Mum was initially quite shocked and tried to reassure him and sent him off with me as usual saying that she would have to talk to her husband about it and let him know in the evening. Well, the outcome wasn't at all what I could have predicted. Dad asked us all to come into the kitchen that evening and said how he wanted us all to hear what he had to say.

'I have heard that one of you has asked to leave the farm and the comparable safety of it after one near bombing miss, in the whole duration of the war.'

He then said in no uncertain terms and in an ice-cold manner that if anyone wanted to leave then he would personally help them pack a suitcase and he would take them to the local authorities and leave them there.

'Is that understood? I have provided for you all, put clothes on your back and provided a safe haven for you. Most of you have reacted well and done your best to help out with the war effort, many exceeding expectations beyond your years. I do expect the same from all of you all, is that clear and understood? You're all capable of doing a good job,' he thundered and banged the table.

'Man up,' he said, 'all of you.'

I could see Martins' lip quivering a bit but he never said a word. He went to school the next day and the next, really buckled down around the farm and later went on to become a grade A scholar and studied at Oxford.

'Anyone want to pack a suitcase?' Dad said, and we all shook our heads.

I remember mum saying later, one of her old sayings, 'you have got to be cruel to be kind.'

Another Christmas was coming up and the war was now a world war, the Japanese had attacked Pearl Harbour with grave losses to the American Fleet. They were caught anchored and with very little warning a lot of the ships were damaged. Roosevelt was President of America and called his nation to arms. I was stunned when I heard the news, and wondered how we could ever win, but at least we knew they were on our side. I asked Dad about it, and all he could advise was that America was a mighty nation and we now had an ally to help us, and we would all fight together to overcome our enemies. He also told me it was vitally important that we all pull together, would all have to get on with things and continue with our work on the farm.

We had another incident shortly after that on the farm when Old Burt came running back up to the farm after going to feed the shires, Wilf and Harry with Becky.

'Is the gaffer in he?' said, 'It's rather urgent mam. It's Wilf one of the shires he has caste himself in the stable. I don't know how he's managed it.'

Mum then told me to go and fetch Dad, 'go quickly I think he's just about to go with Jack in the lorry to town.'

I cut across the farmyard and cut them off as they were about to go out the gate.

'Dad, Dad,' I called, 'it's one of the shires. Burt's been up to say he's caste himself in the stables and wants your help.'

Jack was cautious and said, 'surely it's the vet you need and we should be off any minute.'

Dad turned and said to Jack, 'Go without me. I will have to go and see to the shire first,' and he jumped out the cab.

It looked a grim scene when they both looked in the stables and the old horse seemed to be looking up at them with anxious eyes. Burt went on to say that he'd seen something like this happening to a horse before and they had been lucky that time with securing a rope to the horses back leg and being able to pull him further back into the stall so that he could get up. Could he have permission to try it? Dad wasn't sure it would work, and he said the horse was a very weighty animal.

'Well, I thought that perhaps we could try and if we both pulled we might manage it together,' said Burt.

He was almost pleading with Dad now and I even asked if I could help. Dad told me that the best thing I could do was to keep the old shire calm and even Becky ran forward to stroke his muzzle; they would do the pulling. It only took them a few minutes to find a good thick strong rope and even then Dad wasn't sure it would work, and gathered up a third farm hand in case he needed his assistance as well. Then they secured the rope high up on his back leg.

'Ready?' said Dad, 'heave.'

They were all straining on the rope. Miracles do happen, slowly, oh it was so slow but they were able to pull him out of the corner, just enough for the horse to be able to move and he was up in a moment.

'Oh Dad, he's all right now isn't he, he's alright?'

'Yes son,' he said with an emotion in his voice that I had never heard before.
'Yes, Wilf will be alright.'

Business as usual after that, but I went and found mum and when I told her what had happened, she said I could take a couple of carrots to feed to Wilf.

'It must have been quite an ordeal for him,' she said.

Everybody was pleased. Even Jack when he came back, and praised Old Burt and myself for handling things so well, and that Becky must be a 'natural' with the horses. Rare, praise from Jack!

Chapter 29: Career choices

Occasionally friends seem to drop out of school, and Peter who said he was old enough said he'd enlisted and had signed up for the Royal Air Force. I asked him then if he had any idea as to where he might be going to do his training and told him about the airmen, we had billeted with us who had come over from Canada. I didn't see him after that and when I asked the Headmaster, he said he was being sent off on a ship with a group of other lads to Canada.

'Is it in Nova Scotia?' I asked.

'No,' he said, 'It's a lot further away than that. You do realise It's a lot safer to train young pilots over there, and I gather he's off to Banff in the Rocky Mountains. It's an arrangement that lets the pilots learn in a comparatively safe environment and I think he has the makings of being a good pilot. He told me to keep you informed as I believe you were good friends. Keep that information to yourself now Ken.'

It wasn't long after that he gave us all a geography lesson on North America with an emphasise of the western side of Canada and the Rocky Mountains. It made me realise then just how far he had to travel.

When it was time Mum took me over to Derby for my interview and I was signed on officially and then had to wait for my name to be included in the next group of trainee apprentices. Dad had a few contacts in the village, and he arranged for me to get a lift with one of the engineers who passed us on his way to work. He had a motorcycle and side car, which made it easier for me as a passenger. It seemed strange to be leaving the farm on my first day, and I wasn't sure what to expect. I was going from a very well-structured friendly environment to one I knew very little about.

'You have a lot of knowledge about engineering and what goes on,' Mum said, 'but I'm advising you to keep your mouth buttoned and do as they ask and life would be easier all round.'

I quickly found out what she meant as one of the gaffers gave me a bucket and told me to get a bucket of steam from the engine room. I looked at him quizzically.

But he yelled and said, 'Be off! I am waiting for my bucket of steam laddie.'

Of course when I found the man, he just said 'you're the new laddie? Take it on the chin it's all part of a first day's work,' and he chuckled.

Everybody laughed and they all thought it was a huge joke. I felt humiliated, but then I remembered what mum said, 'keep your mouth buttoned' and I did. It did not stop there, because in the afternoon I was told again by my Gaffer to get a long weight. It was the same scenario as the morning, as I came back empty handed again. Only this time the man seemed to laugh even harder and others around him joined in. It was a long afternoon, and I was glad to be going home, but he pulled me aside just as I was leaving.

'Well done Ken,' he said, 'it's your first day here. All part of the initiation dubbing everyone gets here. Even I had to go through it all on my first day, but if you stick at it, you could do quite well here you know. By the way you are now officially one of 'Henrys' Brat's', it's a name we call our new apprentices. See you tomorrow.'

Come the end of the week though I knew the place like the back of my hand and most of the apprentices names, but the gaffers were the gaffers. And I could manage the tools with an amount of competency being used to doing the fixing jobs that 'E' and I had carried out. Even so the apprenticeship took me two years and the weeks were long, Monday to Friday with a half day Saturday. I had to study hard and sometimes there was even homework. Time was my future and yet to unfold. It seemed strange going to work now, and then coming back to the farm. As if I lived in two worlds. One was the young man finding his way in life, and having to buy my own car magazine, forming a friendship with another apprentice called Alan. And the other beginning to deeply appreciate the steadfastness of the farm life which seemed to flow around me. The good solid plateful of food on the table and supper around the kitchen table. The war continued.

We were also fortunate with farm life because we became fit strong and hardy, and remained healthy as mum put it, although she always made syrups and lotions during the summer, 'Just in case!' she said.

Jacob's scar had healed well although there was still a mark visible, but we had all got so used to seeing it that I don't think anyone took any notice of it anymore.

It was Jack who raised the subject first and asked Dad if he could get his own puppy to live with him in the cottages. He quickly pointed out that the farm dogs, good as they were at their work, were certainly getting on in years, and we needed new blood on the place as he put it. Dad wasn't at all keen as he asked Jack when he would have time to train it.

'I can't have a young puppy roaming about on the loose with chickens in the farmyard and sheep grazing in the orchard. I'm sorry Jack the answer has to be no, though it wasn't a bad idea' he said, 'let's bide our time a bit.'

I am not sure what Dad meant about biding our time a bit, but Jack took him at his word. It wasn't till a couple of weeks later that he returned from seeing one of his friends {and taken Becky} with a young black Labrador puppy, which Becky was holding in her arms.

'He's the runt of the litter and I'm not sure he'll survive but I didn't have the heart to turn down his offer,' he said.

Dad was not happy and took one look at it and said if it survives it will be a miracle and marched out. He'd reckoned without Mum and Becky. It was put inside an old hat by the range and when Becky saw mum feed it tiny drops of warm milk she asked if she could do it too. There was no going around the farm with Burt, not while there was a puppy to feed, and she constantly fed the little pup she had called Butch. Where she got the name from nobody knew, but somehow it seemed to stick. Butch made a fight for his life, and as with all animals under Becky's care pulled through and survived against all the odds. Even mum was surprised. He wanted to follow her everywhere and mum found a collar and lead for him so that they could train him from an early age.

As it happened Dad was spending more time in the kitchen arranging supplies and talking to gramps on the phone. One day he was watching Becky as she burst into tears and told him that Butch was a bad dog and had eaten her slipper. I watched apprehensively as Dad took the situation to hand and authoritatively told her to stop crying and he would show her how to deal with the situation.

'No more tears, that doesn't help!' and then he scooped the frightened young pup up and stroked him quietly. 'Training is what he needs,' he said, 'with lots of love, patience, and treats and a firm manner when he misbehaves.'

Together they took on the training and Butch was a very quick learner, as well as Becky and Jack bemoaned the fact and said that far from him having a new working dog, it was more Dads' dog and a household pet - loved by us all, {including Jack}, and taken on endless walks, especially by the airmen.

It came out in the news about the D-Day landings and forces moved to break the stranglehold of the German empire. Gramps who seemed to be in the know about most things said it had been a very tricky time for the initial launch as they had dropped some paratroopers early on the 5th to secure some of the river crossings behind the Normandy coastline. When the day dawned, the weather wasn't as calm for the special barges to cross the channel so they had to delay the forces until the 6th. Divers that had been specially trained were sent over to clear the underwater defences, and the go ahead was given. Apparently an American general Dwight D. Eisenhower planned the operation from a base in Kent, and allied troops moved in strength for over two months.

The next big event was the bombing of the Eder Dam and the Mohne and I often wondered if that was one of the turning points of the war. They made a film about it later and called it the Dam Busters. The planes had to fly in so low and had a special bomb carriage underneath the plane and when the bomb was released it skimmed the water. And when it impacted on the dam wall was designed to crack and split the wall. The airmen were brave in their efforts and as a result Germany lost it main source of power that they had been so reliant on.

Still the war continued, and the next thing I knew was that Peter had returned from Canada and he told me he now flew a Lancaster, and on his final flights took part in the bombing of Berlin. The airmen came home from their last mission but sadly without one of their number, Carl, who was shot down in the final battle of the war. We all missed him and Jack put a plague on the wall of the cottages after the war to honour his memory. We all clubbed together for it. Butch would often run to the gate as if hoping he would just come back later.

Chapter 30: Then it was over

VE day was amazing, people danced in the street and Mum organised a big street party. There was such joy everywhere. We had won, we had kept our island, and Churchill had led us to victory.

Life continued and although rationing still went on for a while Dad kept the farm going with our produce still going to London, and later on Gramps found new outlets. Jack asked Jacob if he would like to stay on the farm, and be his right-hand man, as he seemed to be able to do most things. Jack also had a word with mum and said if he were to establish his own household, he'd like to have a maid in to keep the place in trim as he put it. Enid asked if she could take on the post as she was fed up with her sisters nagging at her as she put it, and perhaps another sister of theirs could work with Edna. Jack was happy with the arrangement and initially Edna was quite cross with her sister and told her off for getting ideas above her station, her with her lisp, how could she cope? Mum was having none of it and told Enid that Edna was quite capable of the role, so it was then arranged for their other sister Megan to come and help Edna with the cheeses. Of course mum gave her a few weeks to learn the tasks expected of her and she settled in well.

I had worked hard at Rolls Royce and later went on to a managerial appointment and design work on the new models which were always being developed and continued to go to work with the 'gaffer' in his motorbike and side car. Our pick up point changed just before Christmas of 46, as the council stepped in and made some road changes around the village, which seemed to isolate the farm.

True to his word 'E' decided to leave and return to Italy as he had had a letter from his grandfather in Milan. I told him I would miss his company and the times we shared, and he told me to come over and see him.

'Perhaps when you get married!' he said.

Married! I've had enough of Jack's thought's running through my mind, about women, and not being able to trust them. Running off like that with a GI.

'You be careful our Ken,' he'd said.

I did not take his advice too seriously and I grinned at 'E', 'thanks pal we must keep in touch,' and he gave me his address.

He wrote to me after a couple of months telling me he had gone to work in his grandfather's car factory, that he had started in Milan. It later went on to become one of the most prestigious car manufacturers in the world, even to this day, and his grandfather often said he had a natural ability with cars and engineering and wondered where he had got it from. He later went on to the team for design and development.

I still lived at home for a while, and one day mum told me that Becky had asked mum if she could leave school early and look after Burt. He had always been such a strong robust man but when his sister had died shortly after the war he couldn't cope on his own very well and had gone into a steep decline. Mum asked her then if it was what she really wanted to do, and she'd said yes. He'd always been like a grandfather to her, and she couldn't remember her real parents. Then she asked mum if there was any real chance of tracing them. Mum said she didn't think so and told her she was well loved here by all the family and if ever she wanted to come back, she was welcome.
Burt seemed to rally a bit over the Christmastime but come the new year Becky found him sitting in his favourite chair with a peaceful smile on his face. His funeral was a quiet one and when his will was read out, he and his sister had left everything to Becky, 'their beloved grandchild' they'd said. She came back to our house for a while and talked things over with mum as to what she should do. Mum advised her, and said do something that you enjoy doing.

'You have always been good with animals and your marks were high at school, you could still go back to school and get the grades to go to a veterinary college. You have always helped on the farm here and saved many of the livestock that otherwise wouldn't have survived.'

It didn't take her long to decide, and she moved back to her old room at the farm and helped Jack and Dad with the livestock whenever she could.

I left the farm after Christmas and got digs in town nearer to the factory. Come January' 47 the weather changed. It was one of the worst winters that I could remember and started on the 26th. A cold front came in and seemed to settle. Huge drifts of snow were everywhere, the roads were blocked and there were power cuts. I contacted mum and she told me after a weeks snow with no let-up, that Jack, Jacob and Enid were moving over into the main house just to save on the heating.

During the day Becky and Butch helped Jack and Jacob locate the sheep which had been buried under the snow, and they then moved them into the new thatched outbuilding that Jack had built near the cottages. Butch seemed to know where the sheep had been buried and Jack was soon able to dig them out. The chickens which once roamed around the farmyard were rounded up and penned in a section of the old barn with plenty of straw. Dad had to keep the cattle penned in the milking sheds, but it was gruelling work to keep them fed with hay. Production was disrupted for a week, but Jack worked relentlessly on the tractor when he could to try and keep pathways clear, and every morning took a bale of hay down for the shires. It was a hard, harsh winter, and the land was frozen with icicles hanging from the thatching of the barn that Jack had built.

Becky stayed on the farm and was there throughout tirelessly helping mum. Her Butch was the dog that everyone must take with them if they had to go outside.

'Just in case anyone got caught in a whiteout,' Dad said. 'Let him lead you home.'

I privately thought that Dad was being over officious, but I was soon proved wrong. It was Jack who needed him as he slipped off the tractor while dismounting to go to feed the shires. He sprained his ankle and then had to send butch back to the farm hoping he would alert Becky or Dad to come and help him back to the house. When Butch first appeared on his own he barked which was very unusual for him and Mum thought it odd but assumed that Jack was following just behind him. After a minute or two mum realised that Jack was nowhere to be seen and no tractor either. Dad quickly put on his warmest clothing, grabbed a blanket and put Butch on the lead. It didn't take Butch long to get back to Jack and the tractor, but even so Jack was severely chilled by the experience and said it took him ages to thaw out. The cold spell continued.

It was after the thaw in late April there was a report in the paper of a black car which had been left parked up at a local hostelry.

'The driver had never returned,' the paper went on to say that the Police were looking into the incident and could find no trace of the owner. 'Could anyone help?'

I heard later that Dad had found a cap by the riverside at a bad spot, where Jack had extended the gravel path way to past his cottages. It was assumed that someone had got lost and had slipped and fallen in but what they were doing down there nobody knew. The case was eventually closed when a body was found months later. And the coroner recorded a death by misadventure. I asked mum about the incident shortly after when I returned to visit. I had bought my own motor bike by then, so I had my own means of transport.

She said that she had thought it odd that someone should be down there at all. If they had knocked on the door of Jacks house there would not have been anyone there as Jack, Jacob and Enid had moved into the main house when the snow set in. It really was a mystery, on which nobody could throw any light on. I privately wondered if someone had come looking for the old lorry and its contents but as no-one could prove anything I remembered Dad's words of 'what goes on in this house stays in this house,' nothing more was said. It was while I was thinking about the car that I told mum that I was going out to stretch my legs for a walk.

'Take Butch,' she said, 'he can keep you company!'

It was a sunny day, still a bit nippy for April and I reflected on the time 'E' and I spent stripping the old car down and examining every inch of it. When I turned the corner to the lean to I was in for a shock, not only was there no car but no lean to either, and I briefly wondered if I was in the right part of the farm. No, it was the right place but what had happened? The land was flattened. I continued with my walk deep in thought. Jack still had his lorry. I asked him later over supper where he stored his lorry now, and he said he had his own garage for it close to the cottages and went on to say how useful it was and how reliable.

'Not at all like the old car that had been in it at one time. More trouble than it was worth, that was,' he grumbled.

He went on to say that when he had gone around the farm after the melt's as he put it he found the old lean to had just collapsed under the weight of the snow and demolished all that was in it.

'Had to get the tractor out and I took the wreckage down to the old bomb crater. Filled it in nicely,' he said, 'and then I levelled it out. Both sites that is. Mind you I think Jacob rescued an old steering wheel and a cap. Put it on a hook in my garage. It's there if you want it,' he said. 'Useful if you want to build your own car Ken,' and then he turned to mum asking if there were any seconds.

I was stunned, our car, 'E' and I's car, gone. I sat in silence thinking of our loss. As for the steering wheel, I told Jack I most certainly did want it and would go over to collect it in the morning. I felt his empathy. Jacob looked at me and caught my eye, of course he knew exactly what the racing car was.. He knew exactly what it represented being Jack's right hand man. I felt bereft, as if I had lost a precious part of my racing memorabilia. Gutted.

Over the years, I continued to return to the farm and it was on one particular visit that it coincided with Becky's return from the veterinary college where she was studying and we took a walk down to see the old shires, Wilf and Harry. We were easy with each other and shared some of our memories of the war. It didn't take us long to conclude that we were right for each other, but more than that there was something between us like an invisible cord that held us together and we got married six months later. The memories are starting to fade now and I'm back in the nursing home tugging at the suitcase.

Oh yes, the suitcase, the cap, and the letter tucked in the rim.

'Dear Ken,' my mum had written. 'Just writing this for you. I don't know when you will get to read this, but I thought it best to let you know in more detail about the cap that was found by the riverbank in the winter of 47. The worst in my memory. Late one afternoon Butch was very restless and kept on going to the door, and your Dad let him out. He ran off and continued barking but soon came quickly back. It was a few days later that your father found a cap down by the river and took it to the police, and it wasn't until a month later that a body was washed up downstream. Jack was able to tell the coroner as it was on his farmland that the cottages had been empty for nearly two months as he and Jacob had moved into the main farm because of the severity of the winter. The house wouldn't have been occupied if anyone had come knocking on the door. As no-one could give a reason for their visit, - even the landlord of the local hostelry - a 'death by misadventure' was recorded by the coroner and the case was closed. There was no foul play on anyone's part but your Dad did recognise the cap as being identical to the one in the transporter, the foreign one which broke down after the '38 Grand Prix, and housed the racing car the Auto Union. Such memories!'

Copyright E. Robertson 2022

Acknowledgements

My thanks:

To all who have given me encouragement along the way, .

To Douglas Young, Convenor of the Clan Young, Canada, for the remembrance of his relatives, Carl and Tex Livermore and Charles Hugh Winters, the flyers.

To Foley, the British diplomat working in Berlin.

To Ludwig Guttmann the neuro surgeon who founded the paralympic games.

The young lad who worked at Vickers engineering in Tyneside, Mary the student studying in Paris, and the Jewish Sculptor.

Live characters woven into Historical facts and data.

And lest we forget, the warriors who never returned from the conflict.

Roll of Honour

To some of the legends of the sport, to the tracks, the marques, and to those associated with the world of Speed

'Bengy' Benjafield who founded the B.R.D.C. 1928

Mary Wheeler, MBE, who founded the B.W.R.D.C. 1962

Sheila Van Damm, The Dog House – W.M.R.A.C. 1962.

The governing body of motorsport – formerly RACMSA

The places

The Brickyard, Brooklands, Shelsley Walsh, Donington Park, Le Mans, Mille Muglia, Silverstone, Isle of Man TT and the Nürburgring

Some of the faces

Fangio, Nuvolari, Rosemeyer, Raymond Mayes, Caracciola, Jim Clark, John Surtees, Phil Hill, Graham Hill, Nicki Lauda, Sir Jackie Stewart. Jochen Rindt, Jack Brabham, Stirling Moss, Nigel Mansell, Schumacher and the rain masters, Ayrton Senna, James Hunt and Sir Lewis Hamilton.

Ginger Woods, Jimmie Guthrie, Dobson, Barry Sheen, Randy Mamola, Rossi, Agostini, Surtees and Hailwood.

Some of the eminent characters and companies

Colin Chapman, Eddy Jordan, Christian Horner, Murray Walker

Mercedes Benz, Auto Union, Morgan, E.R.A.,Delahey, Bugatti, Maserati, Ferrari, Aerial, Honda, Kawasaki, and Tesla.

Just a few of the many famous names engraved in the history of motorsport.

Summary for book

Life on a rural farm in pre 2nd World War England with its austerities changes when a young boy becomes involved in motor racing at the local Park, Castle Donington. Read how the family adapted, its' Jewish/German connections and its wartime survival.

Powerful cars went to Castle Donnington with their flamboyant drivers, Prince Bira, Lord Shuttleworth, Earl Howe, Billy Cotton (the Big Band leader) to name a few.

Yet as a whisper from down the years rumour has it that not all the racing cars returned to mainland Europe. Myth or Legend or can the final clue provide the answer?

The story slowly evolves around farm life incidences and village life of that era to its conclusion after the second world war.

Printed by Amazon Italia Logistica S.r.l.
Torrazza Piemonte (TO), Italy

48008934R00087